DMcB

The Hunter of
Faro Canyon

The Hunter of
Faro Canyon

Lauran Paine

THORNDIKE
CHIVERS

This Large Print edition is published by Thorndike Press®, Waterville, Maine USA and by BBC Audiobooks, Ltd, Bath, England.

Published in 2005 in the U.S. by arrangement with Golden West Literary Agency.

Published in 2005 in the U.K. by arrangement with Golden West Literary Agency.

U.S. Hardcover 0-7862-7399-2 (Western)
U.K. Hardcover 1-4056-3310-7 (Chivers Large Print)
U.K. Softcover 1-4056-3311-5 (Camden Large Print)

The text of this Large Print edition is unabridged.
Other aspects of the book may vary from the original edition.

Set in 16 pt. Plantin by Al Chase.

Printed in the United States on permanent paper.

British Library Cataloguing-in-Publication Data available

Library of Congress Cataloging-in-Publication Data

Paine, Lauran.
    The hunter of Faro Canyon / by Lauran Paine.
      p. cm. — (Thorndike Press large print Western)
    ISBN 0-7862-7399-2 (lg. print : hc : alk. paper)
    1. United States marshals — Fiction.   2. Large type books.
  I. Title. II. Thorndike Press large print Western series.
PS3566.A34H86 2005
  813'.54—dc22   2004028360

The Hunter of Faro Canyon

Chapter One

THE BIG COUNTRY

The problem was simple and insoluble. Faro Canyon was roughly three miles wide and sixty miles long. There were two cow outfits down there and five or six wild-horse camps. There was no village in the canyon itself, but upon the eastward barranca was the town of Holt. Up there, cattle interests operated all the way easterly to the Liberty River and in two other directions, north and south, from the territorial limits of Arizona to the Mexican Line.

The problem was to find the man named Bart McClelland. His trail had brought the deputy federal marshal right up to the northernmost rims above Faro Canyon. Bart McClelland was somewhere down in Faro Canyon — or else he was upon the huge plateau on the east side of Faro Canyon, and perhaps he was in the town of Holt, but he was somewhere close by and Deputy U.S. Marshal Taylor Hawkin knew it as well as he knew his own name because he had seen the faltering big black horse under McClelland, the last glimpse they had had of one another in this gruelling race away from Wyoming law.

That black horse hadn't gone one step farther than Faro Canyon.

For Taylor Hawkin the chase had to now assume the appearance of a manhunt, and yet he had to be very careful. Among the interesting sidelights of this chase were two factors: one, he had never seen McClelland up close and had only a four-year-old picture from the U.S. Marshal's office back in Cheyenne to go by, in his pocket. Two: McClelland had come from this upended wild and rather desolate northern Arizona area.

Taylor Hawkin did not know a soul down here. McClelland probably had about as many friends or relatives within cannon-shot of Faro Canyon.

The country was big and empty-seeming and because this was springtime there was a fragile kind of very delicate beauty to Faro Canyon as well as to the saffron-shadowed welter of spaced and regulated great craggy mountains all around.

But the world of almost any lawman west of the Missouri was a dangerous place, and when he ventured into areas where there was no law which was not interpreted individually by everyone who owned a gun and a horse — not only individually but usually differently, he steadily increased his chances of never riding out again.

Taylor Hawkin stood at the head of his horse high above Faro Canyon looking in all directions, tremendously impressed by the breathtaking vastness and beauty, and finally decided that here was indeed a place where men had left their bones, and probably had done so with no more than one other person ever knowing where the bullet had found them.

Men like Deputy U.S. Marshal Hawkin developed a 'feel' for a territory, and sometimes they also developed an ability to sense what the outcome was to be of their current assignment. Taylor smoked a cigarette upon the high, shadowed late-day ramparts, completed his study of the new country he was in, shook his head and told his strong bay horse he could feel it — they were riding right down someone's gunbarrel — and swung back across leather to start the hours-long rough descent.

Faro Canyon was long and wide and deep. It was almost a separate world from the upland-plateau country which was mostly free of trees and underbrush, and which was flat and open as opposed to Faro Canyon's many thickets, its stands of forest monarchs, its rushing wide creek and its stirrup-high stands of orchard and wheat grasses. It was almost tropical, and although it did not get sunshine until about ten in the morning, and the sun departed again about three or four in the afternoon, in the summertime it was hot down there, hotter by several degrees than it ever got upon the high plateau.

Two families, the Croslys and the Durants, ruled most of Faro Canyon. They ran their herds down there, patrolled the canyon against trespassers, and whether they had a legal right was seldom questioned. The Croslys and the Durants were a formidable obstacle to any variety of trespassing, but as a matter of fact they were lenient. Usually, at any rate, they were tolerant outfits. They had also been intermarrying at such a rate over the past half century, and healthily reproducing, that neither outfit hired outside riders. They did not have to, there were enough Croslys and Durants to manage the Faro Canyon unfenced, uneven, extremely rich cow country without employing a single import.

They only allowed two big rib-brands in Faro Canyon. A big C and a big D. Any other cattle found in there either fed the Croslys and Durants or were choused down-canyon. Rarely had strays ever been punched back up atop the plateau for a reason: years ago the Croslys and Durants had learned that if they solicitously returned someone's strays to the mesa-cattlemen, they had it to do over and over again. It was always the nature of feed-conscious cowmen to allow as much straying as the neighbours would tolerate.

But if cattle never came back up out of Faro Canyon, vigilance was maintained all around the rims and that accomplished precisely what the Faro Canyon cattlemen wanted — privacy for themselves and for their cattle.

There was no genuine antagonism between the canyon and mesa-cattlemen, but each eyed the other, upon the rare occasions when they met, with candid interest and suspicion. The Croslys and Durants were hard, rough, occasionally violent men, and they shared a sense of loyalty which was remarkable even in a place and a time when loyalty to the brand a man rode for was paramount. And there were a lot of them. No one in the town of Holt had ever more than made an estimate, but it was said there was a Faro Canyon cowman for just

11

about every tree down there.

The marshal of Holt once said they had the most unpredictable men and the handsomest women down in Faro Canyon of any place in Arizona Territory. He should have known, he'd been tangling with drunk Canyon riders since before he'd turned grey, and his wife was a Crosly, one of the few who married up out of Faro Canyon.

There was no way under the sun for a stranger to arrive in Faro Canyon, providing he attempted it in broad daylight, and pass along inconspicuously, and if he remained in the Canyon more than a couple of days he was certain to have someone ride out of the underbrush and confront him.

Most Croslys and Durants were friendly people; at least they offered friendship first, and showed meanness afterwards only if it seemed warranted, by their standards and their rules.

As far as Marshal Frank Beckman of Holt Township knew there had been no outright murders in the Canyon. There had been shootings of course, over the years, and some killings, but neither of the Canyon's clans were skulking people; they might hang a horsethief, shoot down a rustler, or perform surgery upon the attacker of one of their handsome womenfolk, but they were not noted for bushwhacking and in fact they were raised to be scornful of killers.

As a rule they were big, powerful, rough men; not the kind to have to resort to ambushing. When a Crosly or a Durant flung down his hat and spat on his hands there was usually an interlude to follow which was the talk of many a cow-camp cooking-fire for years to come.

Taylor Hawkin was riding from the northward rims down into this insular world of clannishness and privacy. He might have skirted round and come out upon the mesa had he known. He might not have, too. Somewhere, probably down in Faro Canyon, was a man who had shot down a banker and a woman cashier in cold blood back in Denver. Taylor Hawkin had come a very long way to find Bart McClelland.

He did not reach the canyon floor the same day he first saw Faro Canyon from the rims, but he was two-thirds of the way down and that spoke a lot for his powerful bay horse because it was a considerable distance from those northward bulwarks on down to where the grass and trees grew.

He was in the saddle again well before sun-up, and in fact he did not see the sun until quite a few hours later because as it arose, he kept descending. By the time it was flash-flooding the mesa-top with brilliance Taylor Hawkin was down among the horse-sized granite boulders marking the foothills, and an hour later he was out of that tangle as far as the trees and grassland.

Faro Canyon had never been inhabited up where he first entered it, not even by the Indians. Perhaps the ground was too rocky; for a fact the farther down a man rode the better the earth became, but Taylor was a careful man; he did not go exploring, he instead let the horse have its head and when they came to a trickle of water in a grassy place, he made camp even though there would be a long while before evening arrived.

The bay horse deserved this treatment.

The sun soared across Faro Canyon and reached the far side before beginning to descend. It was a lazy, warm day with gnats and mosquitoes and small varmints in the underbrush. Taylor draped saddlebags from a low tree limb, unfurled his bedroll close by an unkempt, fragrant old flowering tree of some kind, gathered faggots for his supper fire and was perfectly willing to take a half day off in his quest.

He thought Bart McClelland had to be no more than perhaps half a day ahead. Back at Denver where Taylor had first taken the trail, McClelland had been two full days ahead. When Taylor had whittled that down to one day, then less than one day and they had both been making good time under the same sun, McClelland caught his first glimpse of the unrelenting pursuit. McClelland at first had not been worried. Later, when he saw Taylor Hawkin top a ridge with a carbine across his lap, McClelland picked up speed. By evening of that day when he could *hear* that burnt-brown man on the strong bay horse, Bart McClelland started using up his horse.

Dead or alive meant a professional manhunter, even if he served the law, had the absolute right to decide which it was to be. Everyone knew perfectly well that many a dead fugitive had been delivered cold and belly-down over leather simply because it was safer to bring him back that way — and a hell of a lot simpler.

Chapter Two

A MEETING

Taylor had a blueprint of Faro Canyon in his mind from the day before up there atop the northward peaks.

He had seen a ranch-yard miles southward. So far southward in fact that he had estimated that it would take a couple of days to reach it.

He had seen no other indication of human habitation but he had seen game-trails and cattle-trails, mostly heading towards the creek or away from it.

The far-southward ranch-yard he had seen was the original Crosly stake-out. He did not see the Durant place which was much closer to the foothill boulder-field because it had been created among forest giants on the east side of Faro Creek with a view to complete seclusion.

It was roughly two miles below where he had camped. Just far enough away and out through the trees across the watercourse so that Taylor did not hear a sound last night when he climbed into his bedroll, even though the Walker hounds of the hunting-Durants had detected his scent early and had consistently bayed.

It was cold when Taylor rolled out to stir his fire and go look for his bay horse. The animal was asleep, full as a tick, and unmindful of everything. Taylor went back to rummage for his soap and head for the creek. He didn't shave; he never shaved on cold mornings alongside cold-water creeks. He usually shaved about midday when things were a little less difficult. But he scrubbed and combed his hair and returned to the fire to start breakfast. He made coffee in a pot not much larger than a couple of fists one atop the other, and sipped that while he worked with more care over the iron frypan.

Only when he looked up, finally, because he'd heard the horse walking into camp, did he decide that dawn light probably never reached down into this place where he was camping, and probably did not reach down into any other part of Faro Canyon.

He did not see the horse; it was moving beyond some huge jumbled boulders so he went back to work making breakfast, and the second time he looked up it was in response to something he had never been able to define. Intuitive warning.

Evidently it hadn't been the bay he'd heard. There was a sturdy girl in her late teens or early twenties leaning both hips against a big rock holding the reins to a black horse and steadily studying him.

She had a complexion like ripe peaches and dark green eyes. Her hair was red-dark and was held severely back from her face by a tiny thong. She was sturdy and muscular.

Taylor finished his study of her then lifted his hat and smiled. 'It's fry-bread,' he announced. 'It's about all I know how to cook very well.' He considered the skillet a moment. 'You're welcome to half and there's another cup of coffee if you'd like.'

She continued to watch him in silence even after he had finished speaking. Then she draped the reins from a crack and strolled closer. She wore black boots and a rusty, split riding-skirt. Her spurs were silver overlaid and had two raised letters upon them: 'B D'.

Taylor filled the cup again and arose to offer it to her. She made no move to accept it so he shrugged, faced her across the fire and sipped coffee by himself.

She said, 'Do you know where you are?' and he nodded. 'Yeah. Arizona.'

'Faro Canyon,' she corrected him.

18

He accepted that. The fry-bread was about ready. He looked down. 'Faro Canyon if you say so.' He knelt and removed the skillet, scooped dirt and doused the fire inside its little ring of stones then he eased back to look up at her.

'Share?' he asked.

She shook her head and moved back a couple of steps. 'Will you tell me what you're doing down here?' she asked.

Taylor pointed with his bootknife. 'Sit. Sure I'll tell you.' He watched her select a place, and lean until the riding-skirt was pulled against a strong hip and thigh before seating herself.

He deliberately cut the pan-sized piece of fry-bread right down the middle, handed her the skillet and the knife, lifted out the half he claimed of the fry-bread and rolled it to be eaten by hand.

'Your name is Barbara,' he said.

She blinked. 'Yes. Barbara Durant. You've seen me before?'

'No. I took a chance on that B engraved on your spur. Barbara, Betty, Belinda, Beulah — I took a chance on Barbara.'

They ate for a moment in silence. He watched her. She was very attractive; in fact if her hair had been put up differently and she'd been dressed differently, she would have been beautiful.

She caught him watching her. 'Tell me,' she ordered, and ate his fry-bread, 'why you're in the canyon?'

'I'm on my way south from up around Denver. It's a trifle early in the season I know, but I figured to take my time and see the country.'

'You've never been down here before?'

'No ma'm. I've been in Arizona before, but a long ways eastward. This is all new country to me.'

'Especially Faro Canyon, and I'll tell you about it.'

She did. She finished eating, handed back his skillet, dried her hands on the grass and told him about the Croslys and the Durants, when their forefathers had first ridden into the canyon back during the Indian troubles, and how there were only people with one of those names or the other one in Faro Canyon. She gave him a very good explanation and she concluded it by saying, 'Mister, we don't hire riders down here and we don't favour gawkers nor campers. There have always been far too many wild horses up and down the canyon so folks have allowed mustanging by outsiders, but that's all . . . I'm just telling you this for your own good.'

He swabbed the skillet with swatches of

grass, cleaned his coffeepot, set them both by his saddlebags and settled back comfortably to roll and light a smoke while gazing at Barbara Durant. Even with no sunlight to strike rusty red flames from her hair and to deepen the emerald of her eyes, she was something any man at all would have thoroughly enjoyed just sitting, and smoking, and looking at.

Every man deserved to have such a vision, such a bitter-sweet cameo tucked away in his mind which would never change and never age; something to refer to in moments when he needed comfort for as long as he lived.

'I'll keep going,' he told her, and grinned crookedly. 'Is everyone down in Faro Canyon this quick to scout up strangers and lay down the law to them?'

'Quick? We knew you were up here before dark last night,' she said. 'The hunting dogs my brothers keep scented you up.'

'How many brothers, Barbara?'

'Nine.'

He trickled smoke. 'How many Durants altogether?'

She pursed her lips slightly before answering. 'It won't make any difference, will it, if you're going to ride on through.'

'No, I expect not,' he replied. 'I wasn't

trying to make you mad. I don't really care how many there are.' He leaned and pushed the cigarette into the mounded dirt over his cooking-fire. 'Do you folks ride out of here very often, and maybe go out to the big cities?'

'No.'

'Strangers ride down in here, then, very often?'

'No.' She sat and studied his face, then she said, 'What's your name?'

He answered truthfully. 'Taylor Hawkin.' It wouldn't have meant anything up around Denver so it certainly wouldn't mean anything in this place.

He rocked forward, shot up to his feet, stepped across the tiny stone-ring to offer her his hand and pulled her up to, then he released her and turned his back. 'Where is the nearest town?' he asked, although he already knew where it was having spied it from the rims the day before.

She pointed. 'Up on the mesa about five miles from here. Can you see that switch-back-trail yonder?'

He turned and looked. 'Yeah. All right, I'll head over there.'

'It's called Holt, for a man who used to have a stone corral up there,' she told him, and moved slightly around until she could see his face again. 'If you wanted to stay in Faro Canyon, no one would really say anything.'

He cocked a blue eye at her. 'That's different from the impression I got a while back, Barbara.' He went on, striking camp, filling his saddlebags, kicking the rolled blankets over closer to the bags and the booted Winchester.

'There are too many mustangs here,' she said.

He straightened up scratching his head. 'Are there?'

'No one among the Durants or the Croslys cares if mustangers come down here; in fact we're glad to have them because they thin out the wild horses and that leaves more feed —'

'For your animals,' he finished for her. 'I'm not a mustanger.' He smiled. 'Wild horses couldn't make me want to stay here, and I guess not much else could . . . but you sure could.'

She stiffened and he had not expected her to react in any other way. He picked up a shank of rope and turned to walk away. 'I only meant it as a tribute, Barbara. I'm not going to come anywhere near you.'

He walked away in search of his horse.

The chill gradually departed to be replaced by a very pleasant kind of shadowy warmth. By the time Taylor Hawkin got out where the bay was and brought him back, the handsome girl and her black horse were gone but that steady increase in new-day temperature did away with the last vestiges of morning chill.

He saddled up thoughtfully dwelling on the peculiar insularity of this place he had stumbled into, and also dwelling upon her answer to his questions concerning others like himself arriving down in her canyon.

If McClelland had actually entered this place, and if he were some way or another related or aligned with these people, no stranger would be able to very easily come in here and find McClelland, let alone ride out of here with him.

Taylor splashed across the creek heading eastward towards the switchback road leading up to the overhead plateau. Twice he started up bands of horses, and both times they were rib-branded, one time with a C and the last time with a D.

He grinned and shook his head. His world was full of hidden canyons, unexplored mesas, emerald meadows and cobalt mountain lakes where people scarcely ever appeared, but this was the first time he'd ever come across an entire vast canyon ruled by its original settlers and their numerous descendants.

The humour did not last long because along with any speculations he was bound to make concerning the inhabitants of Faro Canyon, there was the reason for his presence here.

He knew very well how powerful a commodity loyalty was. If McClelland was over in that plateau cowtown he would be able to breathe a little easier. Not easy, but easier.

Once, he saw several mounted men making a gather of fat redbacks in and out of some tall pine trees, and watched. The cattle knew enough to make a break for it and try scattering throughout the trees. The horsemen tried noisily to prevent this from happening, and for a while it was touch and go, then the riders came out of the trees chousing cattle ahead of them and that ended the game.

A couple of those men saw Taylor in the distance and casually waved. He just as casually waved back wondering whether they were Durants mistaking him for a Crosly, or the other way round.

There was direct sunlight and more heat over closer to the uphill roadway, and what had appeared always before as a snake trail switchbacking its way up across the barranca-face of the high bluff to the town above, turned out when Taylor was close enough to the approaches to be able to see straight up it, to be a wide, painstakingly broadened and shored-up and well-cared for roadway wide enough to accommodate a big freighter or a long jerk-line hookup.

But the grade was bad and nothing anyone could ever do would change that. Hauling a heavy load *up* would be pure hell on a team or a hitch. Going down wouldn't be bad as long as wagoners successfully locked their rear wheels.

For a saddle animal though, the grade was not at all difficult. Even so, considerate livestockmen had carved turn-outs into the face of the barranca at decent intervals.

Altogether, it was a progressive roadway, which Taylor Hawkin told his bay, was a hell of a lot more than he could say for the canyon he was riding up out of.

Atop the mesa there was a light wind coming from the northward mountains. Perhaps when it left the highlands it was pleasant. Maybe by the time it got half way across the plateau it was still pleasant, but when Taylor first encountered it on the stageroad into Holt, the little pleasant breeze had become hot and dry and un-pleasant.

Holt was one of those towns which was half very old and half rawly new. But it at least had shade trees, thanks to someone long dead, and it had plenty of water which was also a blessing, so Taylor Hawkin entered it finding things to like right from the start.

He left his bay at the livery-barn with explicit instructions about a bait of grain, a flake of clean hay, and a cool stall to be cuffed down in. Then Taylor went in a beeline for the saloon which stood opposite the town's general store.

So early in the day he had almost the entire bar to himself. He appreciated that; this was the first drink he'd had since Denver. In many ways that was the same as saying it was his first drink in half a tired lifetime.

Chapter Three

TOWNSMEN

The saloonman was one of those gregarious individuals in whom tact had been instilled over a period of years as a saloon-owner. He only indicated by one remark that he recognized in Taylor Hawkin a stranger to the town and perhaps the high mesa.

He said, 'Usually, first thing a feller does when he hits Holt this time of year is head for my place.'

Taylor sipped his drink. 'It's the only saloon,' he explained.

The barman was greying and scarred, burly and rugged. Clearly, he hadn't always been in this trade; he looked to Taylor more like a thick, oaken freighter, or perhaps a blacksmith who had moved up from soot and clinkers. His name was Preston Lynch, but at this time Taylor neither knew that nor especially cared about it. The beer was seasoned, for a change, and it lacked the bitter taste of most home-made beer. In fact Taylor had his second glass of it, then paid an honest compliment.

'Damned good. Best I've had in months.'

The scarred and rugged man smiled. He had heard this many times before. 'It's in the amount of hops you use, mister. If you don't like bitter beer, why then you got to filter that bitter taste out. Me, I like a smooth going-down beer.' He was polishing glasses as he stood talking. He studied Taylor. 'But it's stout, friend. You keep on drinkin' it down like that, and directly you won't be able to find your behind using both hands.'

Taylor had already noticed. He made the second glass last.

'Riding season opened up around here yet?' he asked, knowing in advance the answer.

'Directly,' stated the barman. 'Yeah, I think some of the outfits are commencin' to hire on.' He placed a polished glass along his backbar and admired the shine before also saying, 'Just don't go down in that broad canyon yonder lookin' for work; it's run by two families that are so interbred it's a blessed wonder they don't all have hairlips. And they don't hire outsiders.'

'Closed territory, eh?' Taylor mused.

The barman faced forward to finish drying glasses. 'Mister, around the mesa up here they got a saying that Hell itself ain't half as exclusive as is Faro Canyon.'

A large, rawboned man entered who, in some ways resembled Taylor Hawkin, except that he was older and there was a badge on the outside of his butternut shirt.

He came over, nodded at Taylor with an expression of interest, then said, 'Pres, you seen Jake in here this morning?'

The barman turned to line up another shiny glass while replying. 'Nope. He's never come in here before mid-afternoon, Frank.' The barman turned back. 'Something wrong?'

The lanky lawman said, 'Give me a beer,' and turned back to looking more closely at Taylor Hawkin. 'You're goin' to beat the ridin' season by a nickel's worth,' he conjectured.

Taylor nodded. 'So I've been told, but hell, there must be more early worms showing up.'

'A few,' conceded the constable. 'Worn-down man on a big breedy black horse came in here yesterday morning, early, like he expected to be the first hired tophand. You're right, there'll be some early worms.'

Constable Beckman hoisted the glass of beer and gazed dispassionately at the barman. 'You're a nosy cuss,' he quietly announced, upped his glass and drank deeply.

Pres winked at Taylor Hawkin and continued complacently to polish his glasses.

Taylor gave it up after that second glass, went out into the midday brilliance and when he looked westward he could see the farthest continuation of the high mesa without being able to see down into Faro Canyon. It was an unusual effect; as though Faro Canyon did not exist.

He rolled a smoke. Around him Holt was busy, but probably not as busy as it would be in another four to six weeks when the riding season was in full swing. There was indication that the cow outfits were preparing themselves for that time. Within fifteen feet of each other stood three big old battered ranch wagons, lined up at the plankwalk across the road at the general store, and out back at a high log dock was a freighter off-loading.

In one door and out the other door — with a slight pause to note the mark-up in between. Taylor smiled to himself. Back up in Denver his family had been in the general merchandise business — the 'emporium' business — since his grandfather had first ridden in with seventeen pack mules to do business with Indian trappers. In fact Taylor's brother still operated the store in Denver.

He walked nonchalantly in the direction of the livery-barn. Two men down there were trying to improve the disposition of a young stud-horse by yanking on the lead-shank and swearing heartily at him. They weren't doing too well. The liveryman walked out. He was a heavy man with a fine paunch and rheumy-looking muddy dark eyes. He hadn't shaved recently and it did not appear that he had changed his attire recently either, but when he went over to the squealing, striking, snorting young stallion and growled at the men on the lead-shank, then went down the rope hand over hand, he calmed the stallion in one minute flat.

Then he turned, spat amber and glared. 'You boys want to make a horse look bad, don't do it in my yard. Folks already think I'm measly. This sort of thing don't help.'

The liveryman stalked back towards the gloomy doorless front entrance to his barn and saw Taylor half-grinning. The liveryman said, 'Gawddamned rangemen. There ain't nobody alive knows less about horses than cowboys.' He paused, then also said, 'And there's plenty of 'em don't know much more about cattle!'

Taylor laughed. The liveryman had to believe Taylor Hawkin was a rangeman. He looked it and he dressed it.

The unprepossessing liveryman continued to glower from beneath thick, salt-and-pepper eyebrows. 'You care for a cup of coffee?' he asked, and led the way to his harness-room/office without awaiting Taylor's response or looking back to see whether or not Taylor was following.

The harness-room smelled powerfully of horse sweat and leather, a pleasant odour at least to people who had matured around it. Otherwise, the room had a desk, two chairs which had once been cane-bottomed but which now had strips of uneven rawhide forming the seats, and a pile of ancient horseblankets beside the desk upon which boxes of fly-specked papers had been piled.

Coffee was made upon a little round wood-stove near the door, and the tin cups were clean, which surprised Taylor. As the liveryman passed over a cup he said, 'My handle's Pete Wintering.'

As Taylor accepted the cup he gave his name, and briefly gripped the fat paw offered him, then he tasted the coffee, and the liveryman watched. 'Pretty good, eh?'

Taylor shook his head. 'Awful.'

Pete Wintering nodded and stepped to his desk to ease down. His face mirrored no realization that his coffee had just been insulted. Instead, he motioned to the other rawhide-seated chair as he said, 'That's one hell of a bay horse you ride.'

Now, finally, it dawned on Taylor why this disagreeable-looking heavy-set individual had been so friendly. Taylor put aside the bad coffee. 'He's not for sale, and yes, he's a good horse.' Taylor eyed the shrewd little pig-eyes of Pete Wintering and the hard-set wide mouth. Overweight or not, this was a man to avoid trouble with.

Wintering shrugged. 'All right. He's not for sale. For a fact that's what I had in mind. I know a cowman east of here who'd allow me to make a little money on a horse like that.' Wintering dropped his head a little to one side. 'You play poker and pitch dice by any chance?'

Taylor's grin returned. 'No. But if you got a horse as good you want to put up . . .'

'Yeah?' said the fat man, leaning a little.

'I'll run you a foot race for them both.'

Wintering eased back looking annoyed. He set his cup upon some papers atop the littered, unkempt desk. Apparently, judging from other rings from wet coffee cups this was not the first time he'd done such a thing.

'You want a job?' he asked. 'Ridin' season don't really and truly open up around here for maybe another five weeks. Meanwhile a feller's got to eat, don't he?'

'I'll manage,' said Taylor. 'Thanks all the same.'

Wintering sighed loudly. 'I'm just plain not going to make a damned dime off'n you, am I?'

Taylor wanted to laugh. Wintering was one of those people whose face mirrored almost every thought as it formed up in their heads. Right now he was looking almost mournful.

'You got that black horse looking any better today?' Taylor asked casually, and the liveryman frowned at him.

'What black horse?'

'The one,' lied Taylor Hawkin, 'I saw a feller ride in here yesterday morning. Both of them looked wrung out and used up.'

Pete Wintering's face cleared instantly. '*That* black horse,' he exclaimed, then thought a moment. 'You know, Mister Hawkin, there'd ought to be a darned law against folks being allowed to use up an animal like that. No excuse under the sun to abuse a good animal just because he's decent to you and willin'. Don't you agree?'

Taylor agreed, but he also had one reservation: there *had been* an excuse for the rider of that black horse to use it up; a federal marshal was on his trail and he had known it.

Pete Wintering heaved up to his feet, inspired to this by his indignation. 'Come along, I want to show you something,' he said and lumbered out of the harness-room leading the way.

The black horse was still tucked up, but he looked sufficiently recovered to be interested when two men came to lean on the half-door of his cool and shadowy stall.

Wintering pointed. 'You see that little bandage? Well, there was a splint starting. No excuse for a splint on a horse like this — unless he gets abused all to hell — no excuse at all. Well, me'n my nightman doctor a little. We got a poultice that'll prevent splints from showing up providing we can get to them early enough.'

Taylor was impressed. He'd seen many splints in his time but this was the first time he'd ever talked to anyone who had a way of preventing them from standing out and hardening-up.

And of course maybe Wintering's method didn't work, but Taylor's judgement of the fat livery-barn owner was that Pete Wintering made no claims he could not support.

Wintering leaned and scowled and thrust

out his lower lip as he looked the black horse over. 'Two-thirds thoroughbred or I'm a Dutchman's uncle; run like the wind, forage in the brushy foothills, tractable as they come, and young. Just an all-round fine animal, don't you agree?'

Taylor nodded. This was the nearest he'd ever been to Bart McClelland; this close to his horse. He said. 'Where is the feller who owns him?'

Wintering pitched up fat shoulders and let them fall. 'Around somewhere; ain't been in today at all, as far as I know, and hell, that's a fine way to look after a horse you've over-rode.'

Taylor Hawkin had a peculiar sensation between the shoulder-blades. He'd had it before, so he very slowly turned.

The man standing back there in the dinginess was tall and dark and whiskered. He had eyes like wet stone, wet *dark* stone, and he wore his ivory-butted Colt in a flesh-out holster tied low on his right leg.

Even that old picture Taylor carried of this man which showed someone clean-shaven and younger-looking, had to relate to the living prototype because bone-structure, general appearance and colouring could not change very much in that period of time.

Bart McClelland!

Taylor heard the liveryman's sharply indrawn breath. Wintering had made some unkind remarks about the owner of the handsome black horse; if McClelland had been standing back there in the shadows long enough to have heard those remarks, almost anyone would have agreed that the look of frank hostility on his face now, would be justified.

But Taylor had a different idea. McClelland was not looking at the fat liveryman. He had almost totally black eyes and they were fixed unwaveringly upon Taylor Hawkin.

Chapter Four

THE WAKE OF A KILLING

Pete Wintering disclosed a facet of his disposition that quite probably very few people had ever witnessed because sometimes it was possible to go for years on end without making disclosures of deep-down inherencies.

Wintering made that sharp sound of indrawn breath, because he had been astonished to see the owner of the black horse standing back there; he had been completely surprised, but he was not the least bit afraid. In fact, before McClelland had a chance to snarl, Wintering spoke out first.

'I was showing this feller a bandage I put on your horse,' he told the black-eyed, dangerous-looking man. 'And I was telling him there'd ought to be a law against anyone abusing an animal like you done with this one.'

Wintering was absolutely fearless even though he did not carry a sidearm.

The black-eyed outlaw ignored Wintering. 'You,' he said to Taylor Hawkin, 'was askin' about the owner of the black. I heard you do it. And Pres Lynch at the saloon told me a little while back about the stranger come in for a couple of beers.'

Taylor was unimpressed — yet. 'What of it?'

'Mister, I seen that bay of yours. I crawled back evenin' before last and spied him out. I never found your camp or damn you, you wouldn't be here now. *I know who you are!* You lousy bastard, I told Barbara who you was and to let me know when you come down into the canyon. You got past her, but not me — you didn't get past me. Well, where's the badge?'

Pete Wintering turned slowly to stare at Taylor, but the liveryman was not Taylor's immediate worry. He wasn't even armed.

Taylor could have strung out a series of epithets. Of course he'd realized the fugitive-outlaw had known there was a rider coming down his back-trail. McClelland would have been just as carefully looking and en-quiring as Taylor had been, but the way Taylor had envisioned it working out, since he'd kept his identity a secret, was that *he*, not Bart McClelland, would find the man he was looking for.

Wintering started to speak. McClelland's right shoulder sank just a fraction which was

40

what Taylor had been intently watching for. Taylor stepped sidewards, twice, and fired dead ahead, to his left a fraction.

McClelland did not complete the draw. In fact when impact sledged him against a stall-front his hand was flung back by instinct to break the fall and the gun he had been drawing dropped back into its holster.

Then McClelland sat down and folded over.

Horses snorted in fright, gunshot-echoes ran up and down and out of the runway into the daylight, and acrid gunsmoke lingered heavily in the cool, horse-scented barn air.

Wintering was staring across where the dead man still hung half in a seated posture. 'My gawd,' he murmured. 'He's killed.'

A wiry small man scuttled in from out back with enormous eyes and an ashen face. He was clutching a four-tined manure fork. He looked, then whisked away, out of sight again.

Taylor Hawkin walked over, lifted away the ivory-stocked gun of the killer-outlaw, shoved it into his waistband, holstered his own weapon and turned to face Wintering.

'You saw him start his draw.'

Pete shifted his attention. 'You got a badge?'

Taylor fished it out and palmed it for the fat liveryman to inspect, then re-pocketed it as the liveryman frowned at him. 'Well, why in hell didn't you say so?'

Taylor bobbed his head in the direction of the corpse. 'That's why. That, and I didn't know how this town would react. Lots of places are antagonistic to federal officers.'

Wintering stepped back and leaned along his wall. 'Mister, you're *in* such a place. Well, maybe not the town, and maybe not altogether the mesa folk, but by gawd down in Faro Canyon . . .' He glanced again at McClelland and dolefully wagged his head.

Taylor, sensing something, said, 'What's this got to do with Faro Canyon?'

'All I can tell you for a fact,' explained the unhappy liveryman, 'is we got to drag him out of here.'

They both turned as someone's hard, sharp footfalls became audible.

Constable Frank Beckman walked in from out front. There were several other men out there, but Frank had growled at them so they were hovering like vultures along the shaded barn wall out front, peering in and muttering back and forth, but not offering to intrude. Frank was a good-natured, even-tempered man most of the time. Folks knew when not to annoy him. This was such a time.

As he approached, Taylor pulled out the ivory-stocked Colt and offered it but Frank simply looked from the weapon to Taylor, then on around to the incongruously half-sitting dead man, and said, 'What happened, Pete?' He ignored Taylor.

Wintering explained in grunted sentences. 'It happened awful darned fast, Frank. Me and this feller was talking about that dead man's black horse. In this stall, here. We didn't know he come up behind us. Heard us, I guess. But that's not what had him ready for war. This other feller is a federal deputy marshal. That dead feller called him. And by gawd, Frank, he wasn't even in the same class. He never in his life made a bigger mistake.' Wintering turned aside to expectorate amber from his pouched cud of tobacco. 'Fastest killing I ever saw.'

Constable Beckman eyed Taylor Hawkin. 'You got proof who you are?' he asked, and finally accepted the ivory-stocked sixgun, then he studied Taylor's badge, and pursed his lips. 'You got orders?' he said.

Taylor had; he also produced them, and Constable Beckman read them, handed them back and said, 'All right, Marshal. Who is this feller?'

Taylor explained and even showed the copy of the robbery and murder report he carried with him, signed by the district U.S. Marshal up in Cheyenne.

Beckman's stiffness did not depart even though he gradually fit the pieces into a pattern he could believe and accept. He looked past to the liveryman. 'Did you pick up anything about this McClelland feller, Pete?'

Wintering's answer was not supposed to have significance to a stranger, and perhaps if Taylor hadn't come into the country by way of Faro Canyon, it wouldn't have.

'He mentioned Barb Durant, when they was gettin' ready to fight. Said something about knowing her or talking to her, something . . .'

Frank Beckman gazed flintily at Wintering. 'He's maybe one of them, then?'

Wintering answered irritably, 'How the hell would know? I never seen this feller — *either* of these fellers — before in my life. But Frank, you'd better sure hope he ain't a Durant masqueradin' under that other name.'

Beckman made a prophetic comment. 'Not me, Pete. This federal lawman here, he's the one better pray to high heaven he didn't kill a Durant.'

Beckman considered the ivory-butted

Colt, then looked at Wintering again. 'Any other witnesses; was your dayman around, by any chance?'

'No. He come in for a fast look afterwards then rode back out again.'

'You're the only witness, then.'

Pete frowned a little. 'All right. Why are you making it sound like it's something criminal?'

'Was it a fair killing, Pete?'

'Yes, and I already told you that, Frank. McClelland or whatever his name was, was ready for a fight when we turned and seen him standing back there. I told you — he wasn't in Mister Hawkin's class.'

'The reason,' explained Town Marshal Beckman, 'I'm asking you again, is because we got to have a coroner's hearing. That is the law, and you know it, you've been on coroner's juries before.'

'Frank, what in hell is your point?'

'You're going to be called to stand up at the hearing, Pete, and say Marshal Hawkin killed this man fair — and if he happens to have been a Durant, you're going to be saying it in front of every Durant who'll ride in for the hearing that their kinsman — if he *is* one — was shot down in a justifiable shoot-out. I've seen this happen twice before in thirty years. Both times the

Durants didn't like it at all.'

Wintering finally had his answer and he did not look as though he were too pleased, himself, but all he said was, 'Well, I'm not going to lie, Frank.'

Beckman was satisfied on this score. 'I know that. Well, I'll go get a couple of fellers to haul McClelland up to the ice-house until we can plant him.' He turned, looked for a moment at Taylor, then walked back up out of the barn over the same route by which he had entered it.

Taylor made a smoke and lit it. He turned so he would not have to watch as a pair of burly townsmen came with an old grey blanket, rolled McClelland upon it and grunted as they hauled the corpse away.

There had been a fair-sized crowd out front, earlier. By this time, a half hour after the killing, it had thinned down to about a dozen hard-headed loiterers who would stand out there to catch a close glimpse of the killer if they had to stand there all day.

Taylor went back to the harness-room with Pete Wintering and what had originally started out as a casual acquaintanceship, had by this time, without any inkling to either man that such a thing were possible, become almost a physical alliance.

Wintering shook his coffeepot and poured

two cups full of oily looking tepid black coffee, but he left the second one sitting there for Taylor to pick up or leave as he saw fit, while Pete took his cup to the desk with him and sat down.

Taylor ignored the coffee and plugged out the spent brass casing from his gun, pocketed it, plugged in a fresh load from his belt and raised quizzical eyes. 'I'm sorry. I sure never meant to get you into this. For that matter, I sure never meant to meet McClelland when I came down here.'

Pete said, 'Yeah? But you come down here to find out about the feller who owned that black horse.'

That was true enough. 'Yeah. I've been after him since the bank robbery and the two murders in Denver; since two days after those killings, but I had no idea . . . I never had a manhunt turn out like this before — so darned fast. One hour I rode into Holt and the next hour I've got him — but he's dead.'

'So'll you be, if he's a Durant, Marshal. Maybe I'll be too, for testifyin' it was a fair fight.' Wintering sipped his embalming-fluid coffee.

Taylor thought back to the handsome girl in Faro Canyon. She had known, then, that Bart McClelland had passed through, but that only interested him in an oblique manner; if McClelland had been a Durant, or maybe a Crosly, why hadn't he stayed down there where Taylor Hawkin never could have got close to him if those cowmen down there learned who Taylor was and what he was after?

'They protect their own?' he mildly enquired, and got a violent response.

'*Pertect* — Marshal, those folks down there don't just *pertect* their own, they got a whole darned army of fellers who'll hang you just for *drawin'* on someone they're kin to. And for *killing* . . .' Wintering rolled his eyes. 'And for bearing witness against one of 'em . . .' He rolled his eyes back the other way. 'If you are a sure-enough federal officer, then you'd better use all the influence you got and get word out of here that you need a regiment of soldiers. Quick!'

A slightly stooped individual with piercing pale eyes and a slightly twisted wide mouth came to the harness-room and peered past the door without making an effort to enter.

Wintering said, 'Come on in, Jake. Marshal, this is Jake Rowan, stage-company rep in Holt. Jake, this is Deputy U.S. Marshal Taylor Hawkin.'

Rowan, who had a slight curvature and seemed always to be peering upwards as though about to ask a question, shook and eyed Taylor and quietly said, 'I'd of guessed. I saw that dark-lookin' feller as they lugged him past, and I heard the rest of it across at Pres's bar.' He stepped over to look for an empty tin cup to be filled with vile coffee. 'Marshal, that's too bad,' he said, draining the pot and shaking it to make sure it wasn't holding back on him. 'Sure too bad.'

Taylor looked at the stage-company representative unsure of what, exactly, was too bad.

Wintering asked the obvious question. 'What d'you mean — what are you talking about, Jake?'

The man turned, his upward-tilted head slightly to one side. 'That feller's name wasn't McClernand.'

'McClelland,' corrected Taylor.

'Well, whatever folks said it was,' stated Jake Rowan. 'His name was Bartholemew Durant.'

Wintering and Hawkin gazed steadily as Rowan sipped his cold coffee and inquisitively looked from one of them to the other one. 'Ain't that something though? Mister, you killed a Durant.'

'Who says so?' growled Pete Wintering.

'Custer was in my corral-yard with me

when they took that dead feller on past,' stated the stage-company man. 'Cus Durant, Pete, you know him.'

Wintering looked bad. 'I know Cus Durant, yes, and he saw that dead man?'

'Yes.'

'What did he do?'

'Looked real hard. Made those fellers stop until he could peel back the blanket and look real hard, then he bawled out a bunch of cuss words and run out to his horse.' The man with the crooked shoulders finished his coffee. 'You saw the killing?' he said to Pete, and didn't wait for an answer. 'Listen, Pete — don't you bear no witness . . . Marshal, I'm sorry to have to say this. In front of you anyway. Pete, Frank told me you saw the fight and called it fair. You better not say anything that crazy when they have the coroner's hearing.'

Jake peered upwards, around, then put down his tin cup and walked out of the harness-room.

Chapter Five

CRISES

Town Marshal Frank Beckman crossed from Pres's saloon to his combination front-office and jailhouse just before dusk, and met the stranger down there leaning upon an overhang upright smoking and gazing out over the town.

Frank opened the office door without a word and nodded for the Deputy U.S. lawman to enter first, then Frank went in, and kicked the door closed as he headed for his desk-lamp and leaned down to raise the mantle.

'He wasn't named McClelland,' said Frank Beckman. 'By now I expect you know that.'

Taylor knew it. 'Yeah. Feller from the corral-yard said so.'

'Jake,' agreed Constable Beckman, waiting to make certain the wick would burn before lowering the mantle. 'Jake Rowan.'

'Yeah.'

Beckman turned, looked for the hook and

hung his desk-lamp from an overhead ceiling baulk, then pitched aside his hat and motioned Taylor to a chair as he went behind his table.

'Marshal,' he said, 'I guess about the worst thing would be for you to try and ride out of the country.' Frank eyed his guest a little sceptically. 'I'm not saying you got that in mind. All I'm saying is that by now, this evening, they know down in Faro Canyon you killed a Durant. If you try to ride out of here they'll run you down and if it's some miles away from town there's nothing I can do to help you. They'll hang you sure as gawd made green apples.'

Taylor was a little angered. 'If you think I'm going to run, think again, and if the Durants have to make something out of a killing in self-defence, I can't stop them.'

Frank sighed. 'You sure can't, Marshal.'

'Do you know Barbara Durant?' asked Taylor, and the lawman nodded.

'Yeah; in fact she'n my wife are related. My wife was a Crosly. She had a daddy who was a Crosly and a mother who was a Durant, you see, and Barbara is a sort of niece — I'm told. It's kind of complicated. Anyway — what about her?'

'I fed her breakfast this morning and we talked a little.'

'Where?' asked Constable Beckman.

'In Faro Canyon.'

Beckman acted surprised. 'The hell. I figured you'd arrived in town from the north mesa.'

'I rode down through Faro Canyon on McClelland's trail, spent last night down there, talked to Barbara this morning, and rode on up out of there to this town after she showed me the road. Constable, if she knew McClelland — or Durant — rode through ahead of me, she never mentioned it.'

Beckman looked sour. 'Are you implyin' something about aiding and abetting? If you are, Marshal, take my word for it — that's the *least* of your problems right now.'

'That's not what I was talking about at all,' stated Taylor, becoming increasingly annoyed at this attitude everyone seemed to have that he was only a very short while for this world. 'What I was thinking was simply that maybe McClelland didn't come up out of there it all. Maybe he somehow or other swung around and reached Holt without maybe more than skirting Faro Canyon.'

'What of it?' asked Frank Beckman. 'What's that going to do towards helping you out for the killing?'

'I don't know,' exclaimed Taylor, 'and I'm getting damned sick and tired of everyone looking at me like they're measuring me for a pine box.'

'Wait,' cautioned Constable Beckman. 'Just wait, Marshal. There's an army of them down there. They'll be coming maybe in the morning. No later then tomorrow afternoon or evening.'

Taylor got to his feet. 'Are you afraid?' he demanded curtly.

Frank looked and pondered, and did not offer a direct answer. 'Marshal, if the son of a bitch just hadn't tried to out-draw you.'

'What kind of an answer is that?' demanded the federal officer.

'Better'n the truth, maybe,' stated Beckman laconically, and began searching his desk-drawers for a tobacco sack. 'Marshal, I'm not too concerned over what happens to you. I'm not even too concerned over what might happen if some of the Durants and Croslys find you, get you into a corner and force another drawing-match — even though my wife'll be worried sick. What I'm concerned about . . .' He found the sack and leaned back to start manufacturing his cigarette and did not lift his eyes to Taylor's face. 'What I'm plumb concerned about is my town. You see, the liveryman for one — Pete Wintering — and the saloonman for another — Preston Lynch — are the kind of fellers who wouldn't back down from a buzz-saw.'

Taylor frowned. 'What of that?'

'Well,' replied Frank Beckman, then tongued the cigarette paper before folding it deftly and sealing it. 'Well, if someone comes up here from Faro Canyon to make trouble I could have a war on my hands. There are folks right here in town who aren't too fond of those folks from Faro Canyon. There are some mesa-cattlemen who aren't too fond of them either.'

Beckman lit up, exhaled and finally raised his eyes. 'What I want is for you to leave. Get out of my township as quick as you can — any way that you can. I don't want you around here in the morning.'

'A minute ago,' stated Taylor Hawkin, 'you said I couldn't make it.'

'Maybe I was wrong. If you left right now and kept riding right through the night I expect you could make it. I could head off the men from Faro Canyon; delay them for a few hours. Yeah, I expect you could make it.'

Taylor studied Frank Beckman through fragrant blue smoke. He did not know the lawman well enough to make much of an assessment, but he knew *conditions* well enough to think that whether Beckman was deliberately sending Taylor into an ambush or not, if the Durants caught him it would amount to the same thing.

If Taylor Hawkin were overtaken by riders from Faro Canyon miles northward, Frank Beckman could truthfully say he had not known such a thing was going to happen.

But that didn't mean a damned thing to Taylor, the one who would be overtaken and no doubt shot or hanged, so he said, 'Constable, we are the law. You and I are the law. What happened in that livery-barn was perfectly legal and perfectly justified. The law doesn't have to run from anyone — providing it's willing to stand its ground.'

Frank said, 'That's a nice sentiment,' and leaned to dispose of cigarette ash into a coffee tin beside the desk. 'The only way you'll make it work here, Marshal, is if you can bring in a troop of cavalry between now and morning.' The constable arose. 'Mister Hawkin, I'm giving you some darned good advice. I don't want to see a federal lawman killed in my township, and I don't want one to kill anyone else. Listen to me; go north through the mountains and get some support, more lawmen or soldiers or something, then come back.'

Frank Beckman got slightly uncomfortable under the bleak stare of the deputy marshal. He walked to a window and leaned to look forth into the roadway of his town.

In the trade they called it 'temporizing'. U.S. lawmen never ran they 'temporized'. Taylor Hawkin had another name for it. He had never done it before and he had no inclination to do it now.

He left Constable Beckman standing at the window looking out. Elsewhere, the town seemed to have lost some of its customary bustle and vigour. It seemed now to be turned inward, to be more concerned with something which had happened within its limits than with trade or commerce reaching beyond.

Jake Rowan was over in front of the harness shop when Taylor Hawkin crossed the road from the jailhouse, and Jake moved up a few doors to intercept him upon the east side and to say, 'You know what they say the better part of valour is, Marshal?'

Taylor stopped. He hadn't particularly cared for this man earlier, down at the livery-barn, and it had nothing to do with Rowan's way of cocking his head in that listening or cynical posture. 'Yeah, I know,' he answered. 'You know what can happen to folks who butt their beaks into things that don't concern them?'

Jake Rowan blinked and kept silent, and when Taylor walked on, Rowan's thin lips drew flat in an evil expression. He turned and hiked over in the direction of his corral-yard.

At the saloon Preston Lynch seemed surprised but the expression was so fleeting when Taylor walked in it was impossible to say it had really existed. Pres filled a beer glass and shoved it forward before Taylor even got to the bar.

'Beautiful day,' said the hard-eyed, scarred saloonman.

Taylor sighed. 'You're wasting that sarcasm,' he told Preston Lynch, and picked up the beer. They looked steadily at one another until Taylor put the glass down and shoved it aside.

'Mister Lynch, do you know a man named Custer Durant?'

'Sure. So does everyone else in town. What of it?'

'He saw that fugitive I tangled with at the livery-barn when they were carrying him away.'

Lynch said crisply, 'I know that. The feller who runs things for the stage company told me. He was right there. Cus got awful upset and rode for Faro Canyon in a big rush.'

'Yeah, that's right, Mister Lynch. Well, what I'm getting at is: what happens if I don't run?'

'They'll kill you,' stated the barman succinctly, and drew himself a beer too, something he rarely did during working hours.

'And you folks here in town would let that happen?' asked Taylor, arriving at the crux of his purpose in entering the saloon.

Pres Lynch tasted the beer first, then answered. 'You're putting us on the spot, aren't you?'

'I didn't come here with that in mind,' said Taylor. 'But then I didn't come here figuring to have to kill McClelland either.'

'But that's how it happened,' mumbled the burly barman, and sipped more beer while he clearly fumbled with the answer to the question Taylor had asked. 'His name's not McClelland.'

'All right; that's what it says on the dodgers and in my instructions, but I'm willing to use his real name. Mister Lynch . . . ?'

'You ride in here, Marshal, kill a man, arouse half the lousy countryside against you, then come and ask me if I'll help you.'

'No, Mister Lynch, what I'm trying to find out is whether folks in Holt will stand with the law.'

'Did you ask Frank Beckman?'

'Yes.'

'What was his answer?'

'That he wanted to avoid trouble in his township and he thought I'd ought to try and get out of the territory into the northward mountains before they can overtake me.'

Pres Lynch finished his beer and blew out a big breath. 'Bullcrap. They can catch you even if you have as big a head start as that would require, and Frank darned well knows they can. He's married to one — to a Crosly.'

'I didn't have in mind running for it,' said Taylor. 'Even if I figured I might make it, I still didn't have that in mind.'

'No,' muttered the barman, sarcastic again, 'of course not. Why should you try and run for it when the odds are you'll get caught and hanged? If you stay here in town and the Durants ride up out of their lousy canyon loaded for bear you figure there'll be some folks in town who won't be able to stomach those odds. One federal lawman against the men of Faro Canyon.'

Taylor stared squarely at the older man. 'What are my chances?'

'If you stand alone? Not one in a million.'

'No. What are my chances of being

backed up by the people around Holt who'd support the law?'

Pres Lynch said, 'How would I know? I'm just a feller who owns a saloon.'

Taylor waited for more but Pres Lynch had said all he intended to say, apparently, because he took their sticky beer glasses to his sink and dunked them in the greasy water there. He became busy and did not raise his head to indicate he knew anyone was down the bar from him.

Taylor left.

Outside, that peculiar inwardness was still evident. The town was unusually quiet. Over at the big general-store building several people strolled forth, saw Taylor Hawkin in front of Lynch's saloon and paused to quickly speak back and forth, then turn as though they hadn't seen him and briskly head up the plankwalk.

Chapter Six

INTO THE NIGHT

The day ended quietly. There had been a number of stockmen in town, late in the afternoon and through the evening, but for the most part they left shortly after suppertime.

A few lingered, the ones who had come the farthest, along with a few interested and adventuresome souls who had some notion the riders from Faro Canyon might decide to come up to Holt this evening and not wait until morning.

There were two daily stages into and out of Holt. One came from the south in the morning and the second coach arrived from the north in the evening. They had both arrived and departed without anything of much interest transpiring, which was usually the case, and Jake Rowan went home early.

That big freight vehicle which had been out behind the general store since morning, finally completed its business and rolled ponderously down the back-alley on the west side, nearly filling the right-of-way from side to side, and emerged below Wintering's barn where there was ample area for the hitch to be slowly swung out and around. The wagon made it to the stageroad without incident, which was not customary with rigs that big, then its driver lined out his hitch on the southward trace while his swamper, who was little more than a gangling, unshorn boy, sat up there exuberantly playing his mouth-harp.

That music was audible for quite a way.

Taylor ate supper at a small cafe mid-way down the east side, and walked down to look in on his bay horse. There was no one around. The liveryman and his swamper were probably somewhere having supper.

The bay looked fine. So did the big black horse Bart Durant had ridden half to death to reach this country. Someone had removed that bandage from his foreleg and although Taylor did not enter the stall, and the light was not very good from the outside, there did not appear to be any hint of a splint.

Out behind the livery-barn were the public corrals; gnawed and patched, kicked and cribbed until about the only serviceable part of them were the upright posts.

Other corrals, in better shape, belonged

to the liveryman, evidently, because they were adjacent to his barn and were in fact attached to it.

There were a few horses in the liveryman's pens but none in the public corrals.

Taylor turned southward, followed the wide, slick tracks of that freighter's big steel tyres to the edge of town, heard the distant wailing of the mouth-harp, and stood down there in the quickening evening, thinking.

An old soldier had told him once, many years ago, that the reason General Lee had been so successful for so long against the overwhelmingly superior Federal Army, had been because Robert E. Lee was a real genius; he always turned up where he had no right to be.

Taylor walked to the western edge of town, and beyond it a fair distance, until he could feel cool air coming up from Faro Canyon.

It was getting too dark to see much of the view below, and if there was a moon it wouldn't be along until later, like the stars, so all he could really make out was how wide and dark Faro Canyon was from this rim of the mesa above it.

They hadn't arrived tonight so they probably wouldn't ride up out of there until morning.

He rolled a smoke and enjoyed it, thought more about what that old Confederate soldier had told him, and when he finally killed the cigarette and turned back, he walked with a brisk step to the livery-barn and got out his bay, cross-tied it, went after his outfit, and rigged up in the darkness.

He had led the horse out into the rear alleyway before anyone came along. Even then they did not see him because, in the first place, they were not looking for him, and because in the second place it was too dark inside the barn.

But he heard Pete Wintering and recognized the voice as the liveryman said, 'They'll maybe auction him off. That's always been what we've done to pay for burying someone who just arrived in town.'

'Naw,' retorted another voice, more nasal and resonant. 'He warn't a stranger, Pete. You're kiddin' yourself. You're never goin' to get that black horse. Won't be no auction. If he was a Durant them other Durants'll pay for his funeral, and they'll come for the horse as his heirs. You're tryin' to kid yourself.'

Wintering groaned. 'Get the hell to work, and be sure you dung out all them stalls tonight, too, and don't leave it for Arch to do in daylight.'

Taylor smiled and walked away leading his bay horse. He could imagine what would ensue when that nighthawk went to clean the stall of the bay, and found that there was no bay in the stall.

He told his horse that since folks usually believed what they wanted to believe, by the time he rode back to town they would all be convinced he had made a run for it.

There was nothing out beyond town on the western mesa, not even any town milk-cows which were usually allowed to graze back there in daylight. He rode across a lot of empty territory to reach the road leading into Faro Canyon, encountered no one, and hung back atop the mesa for a while, listening. If there was anyone coming up he could not detect them, and if there was it certainly was not any body of riders, so he edged over the lip and started down.

Instantly, he and his horse felt the change in temperature. It wasn't cold but it was cooler than it had been atop the mesa.

The darkness, too, seemed deeper the farther down he went, but shortly before he reached the bottom starlight enhanced by moonlight brought a new kind of ghostly visibility, and that helped.

He didn't really have a plan in mind, although he was not totally without a goal either, but since he had not cared to make a lot of enquiries around town, now he was back in Faro Canyon, probably the worst place for him on earth, with only the sketchiest idea of how the land lay, and where he was going.

Barbara had mentioned dogs hearing him from where she lived the night before they met. He deduced from this that the Durant ranch-yard had to be maybe a mile or so south of where he had camped. Because there had been dark mud on the fetlocks of her horse, meaning she had crossed Faro Creek to reach his camp, she probably lived on the east side and that was at least favourable because he was also on the east side, when he came down off the mesa.

He rode thoughtfully and slowly. Where the trees were thickest he skirted around, but where they had been thinned out he passed right on through, and what finally told him what he wanted to know was a tangy smell of woodsmoke on a low little drifting breeze. It had the faint good scent of cooking to it.

Mindful of those dogs she had mentioned he looked for a place to hide the bay, and finally left it tied where that little breeze blew against it. Of course the breeze could shift, could in fact reverse itself and if it did that, the dogs would surely pick up the horse-scent, but whether those dogs would bark just on horse-smell was doubtful. But they most certainly *would* bark on horse-scent mixed with the scent of a strange man.

He left his Winchester in the boot. He hadn't come here to fight, and even if that unpleasant course were thrust upon him in the darkness, probably at close quarters among big trees, a carbine would be more of a liability than anything else.

He had the full night ahead of him, but that was only one reason for being slow and very deliberate. He also had the whole clan of these people he was looking for fired up to murder him. At least that was the consensus up atop the mesa, and while Taylor did not put all his faith in Constable Beckman, he came pretty close to putting it in Preston Lynch, who had told him he didn't stand a chance against the Durants.

Under these circumstances not even a fool would have rushed forward.

The cooking-smell grew stronger when he moved a little southward. He was unsure about this because that led him through a thicket of thorny underbrush, and from there through a stand of giant trees, which showed here and there where the axe had been. It seemed improbable anyone lived through here.

But they did.

He heard a dog bark, then whine. He heard a man cough and rattle a tin spoon against a metal pot, evidently feeding the dog, and his last fifty feet through the trees set him back where the shadows were slightly less dense upon the farthest perimeter of a large grassy clearing.

The house was of logs and even by starlight looked as though rooms and whole sections had been added on from time to time until the place must have covered more land than three normal houses used up.

There were two fireplaces with smoke coming from them, but altogether he counted six fireplaces. There were lighted windows all down the side of the house he could see, which was the north wall, and that smell of cooking meat became tantalizingly strong this close to its source.

He had to go right up to the very edge of the forest before he could make out the man feeding the dog, but it wasn't one dog it looked more like five or six dogs and each one was on a chain with a little rough-barked house to himself.

Those would be her brothers' hunting dogs. Right at this minute they weren't interested in anything but being fed.

He finally saw the man. He was thick through, heavy in the shoulders, oaken legged and fair. Being hatless in the starlight let his taffy-coloured hair show to better advantage as he stood near the last dog holding a huge metal spoon in one hand and a large old battered metal pot in the other hand.

She had said nine brothers.

Taylor was as tall as that one over by the dogs, but he lacked a good fifty pounds of being as heavy as this brother was.

A woman's voice called from a lighted doorway. 'Ham, we're waiting on you — as usual.'

The man turned and mimicked the woman. 'As usual. What d'you mean — as usual? Just once I got to feedin' the dogs a little late.'

A man's voice cut in gruffly. 'Hamilton, get your carcass in here!'

Ham moved that time, without any arguing and without any hesitation. As he brushed past the woman she edged out upon the long, planked rear porch. Ham went on in, almost entirely blocking out light when he passed through the doorway.

Taylor held his breath. He recognized the girl even in that poor light and at that distance.

She gazed out where the dogs were gulping food, then she said, 'Sheba; why do you always do *that!*' and walked over to untangle the chain of a Walker bitch.

Taylor moved swiftly, trying to get around to that side of the trees before Barbara finished with the bitch and returned to the house.

He didn't make it. She got the dog untangled and turned back with an exasperated admonition to Sheba, which the bitch didn't heed at all as she lunged for her laden dish. Barbara shook her head.

She stepped up to the porch pulled open the door and vanished.

Taylor felt like swearing. Instead he walked back a short distance and sat down upon a big old punky stump. Ahead of him the dogs were noisily eating and over along the rear of the house lamplight showed orange. He could hear voices. Probably, in a clan with as many members as this one had, a person could hear voices at almost any time of the day or night.

Chapter Seven

THE HUNTER
OF FARO CANYON

As soon as the dogs finished their meal they would certainly react to the scent of the stranger. That many dogs excitedly baying would rouse the dead.

Taylor lingered, knowing better but hopeful the girl would re-appear. When she didn't he finally circled to the network of pole corrals, sturdy enough to hold the wildest ton-bull, and sidled from there to the barn. One of the hunting dogs sat back and howled.

In Taylor's mind there was an embryonic notion, supported by actually nothing factual, that if he could speak to the Durants, could explain, they would not all be against him. Not everyone approved of cold-blooded murder. If he could gain just two or three allies that might be enough to delay or sway the others.

And if *that* didn't work he knew a method

which *would,* but in order to abduct hostages he first had to find them, and secondly he had to capture them.

Another of the hounds howled and lunged on his chain. Someone came out back and swore in a bull-brass voice which had enough deep resonance to carry.

'Shut up you pack of skillet-lickin' good-for-nothing sons of bitches!'

More dogs joined in. Instead of the howling diminishing it increased until Taylor saw two other stalwart men stamp out back snarling for the dogs to be quiet, and when they not only disobeyed but became increasingly agitated, one of those three stalwart men said, 'Damn it, Ham, you'd better set them dogs free. Sure as hell there's a 'coon up a tree close by, or they scent a catamount. Look at 'em!'

One of the other big disgruntled men scowled blackly at the dogs, but did not shout at them again, he instead turned towards the house, 'Charley! Come on! Let's get our guns!'

Taylor did not wait to see whether or not the Durant named Charley would obey. The moment they freed those hunting dogs Taylor Hawkin was going to need wings to get away.

He hurried back to the bay, yanked the

shank loose, turned and lit up across leather in a leap, angled in and out of the dark forest until he broke clear near Faro Creek, and changed course. He did not head for the eastward barranca and the roadway leading up to safety, he turned due southward and kept to the open for a fast mile, then slogged out through creekbank mud into the water and rode another mile due southward in the water.

He did not hear the dogs. Several times he halted expecting to hear them, but there was not a sound. He doubted that he had out-distanced them that much.

The territory southward was less wild, more grassed-over and abetted in its cease-less conflict with trees. Down here, there were a number of bleeder-ditches, not very wide nor deep, leading from Faro Creek off through the grasslands upon both sides of the creek. Someone was interested in building up the yield of the grassland.

He came into a moonlighted little clearing with a three-room log house sitting there, dark and silent. At first, because he was some distance off and the light was poor, he thought the log house had probably been built recently, perhaps to house newlyweds, but when he boldly crossed the clearing and got close, the log house turned out to be very old, abandoned, full of wood-rats, and with a dangerous settling at ground-level and up along the bowed ridge. It was evidently one of the first residences ever built in Faro Canyon. Possibly the first Durant or the first Crosly, had lived here.

He did not tarry. Beyond this clearing he paused again, but there still was no baying of hounds. He halted in this place for a little while, swung off and rested the bay's back.

Thinking back, he remembered Barbara saying that the dogs had howled when they'd picked up his scent the first night he arrived in Faro Canyon.

But she had not come to investigate until the following morning. That, he told himself, was it: they knew the dogs had picked up a powerful scent close by, but they would not get on the trail until morning. Maybe this strategy had something to do with daylight offering better visibility. It didn't matter, as long as he understood.

He turned, reins in hand, and walked on southward watching the land open out, become moonlighted and ghostly silver from starshine as the stands of big trees steadily drew farther back upon both sides of the creek.

People had put in a lot of back-breaking days making these formerly forested wastelands turn lush with Dutch clover, broom and orchard grasses, and with varieties of native feed he was not familiar with. The impression he'd been forming since yesterday about the Croslys and Durants being wild, fierce, hard-riding canyon cattlemen evidently was not correct.

At least it evidently was not *totally* correct.

He paused at a little ditch to slip the bridle so the bay could drink, and had both hands high refitting the bridle when a soft voice boomingly said, 'That's just fine, stranger. Just hold 'em up there steady as stone!'

He heard the gun-hammer haul back to full-cock.

With both hands up, ludicrously holding the bridle, he turned his head a fraction until he could make out the thick, bareheaded man standing down-ditch a short distance away, blue-steel in his right hand, up, cocked and aimed.

Hamilton! He recognized the taffy hair in the moonlight and the general thick-through build. He turned fully to stare.

The man stepped over the ditch, trod softly in grass until he was close, then he leaned for a close look, and, apparently satisfied, he shifted around behind to lift away the gun in Taylor's hip-holster.

Finally, Hamilton Durant, stepped back and eased down the dog of his Colt and leathered the thing. 'Finish bridling,' he said, his voice perfectly calm, almost amiable.

Taylor was encouraged. As he worked with the bridle he said, 'What's wrong with someone crossing through, down here?'

Ham Durant answered in the same calm tone, 'Nothin'. Nothin' at all, mister. But you weren't crossin' through, were you? Now don't go and lie. We been raised to despise a liar near as much as a thief.'

Taylor finished with the bridle and turned to look more closely at Hamilton Durant. He already knew the man was thick and oaken and taffy-haired, but now it also appeared in that uncertain light that Ham Durant was also younger than Taylor would have guessed.

'What were you scoutin' up around the home-place for?' Hamilton asked. 'Come on now, mister — remember what I said about lying. Now answer up.'

Taylor agreed. 'All right, I'll answer up. First, how the hell did you get down here so fast?'

Hamilton's big teeth shone in the gloom. 'Well sir, I knew from the tone what my dogs was saying, and you see, there's a passel of us, so we fanned out. I took the south route but I figured you'd be high-tailing it for the road up to the mesa, I didn't figure to catch you. I thought my brothers would. That answer suit you?'

Taylor almost smiled. 'Yeah, it suits me.'

Ham did not smile but his tone remained nearly affable when he said, 'I'm waiting, stranger. What were you doing, scouting up the home-place tonight?'

Taylor considered his options and the one he liked best had to do with saying he'd come back down here to see Ham's sister again. He considered saying it, too, until it occurred to him that by now the people down in Faro Canyon certainly knew the man Barbara had spoken to was also the man who had shot a Durant to death.

Taylor's horse finished at the ditch and tugged his reins. Taylor yielded, moving away from the water with the animal, and when he thought he could cover the distance with some to spare he dropped the reins, sank down on his bootheels and catapulted himself forward. He was not afraid of the un-cocked gun in Hamilton's right fist, nor did he have cause to be. He crashed into the younger man with stunning force and Hamilton staggered. Where another man would probably have gone sprawling, Ham absorbed the strike with bent knees, roared a rough curse and reached his left hand for cloth, but missed and tried clubbing awkwardly with the sixgun, and missed there too because Taylor was already past and turning, and coming up with both fists poised to blast.

Ham turned. Taylor caught him a glancing blow up by the temple. Ham growled, ducked low, tucked his face into the curve of an oaken arm, let go of the gun and went after Taylor crab-like, sidling around sidewards with his right fist drawn back to his right shoulder, ready and aimed.

Taylor feinted, drew the thicker, younger man off-balance, and struck hard. Hamilton kept coming. Taylor stepped to the right, kept manoeuvring to the right until he had drawn the powerful taffy-haired man off guard, and fired again. Hamilton kept coming.

Taylor backed clear, let his arms drop briefly and surveyed his adversary, who was still ponderously walking in, face shielded by the curve of a mighty shoulder, right arm still poised and cocked.

Taylor waited, then ducked far down and shot an overhand blow into Durant's unprotected middle, and this time the inexorable advance was slowed, but when Taylor wanted to repeat that, a big arm was in guard-position.

Nevertheless Taylor knew where Ham Durant could be hurt.

The heavier man bored in again, trying to force Taylor to stand, trying to manoeuvre him into some position where his back would be against an obstacle.

Taylor was lighter, older, and more experienced at this sort of thing. He slid away from each attempt by young Durant to box him in, and each time he came back in a low crouch aiming for the unprotected, vulnerable belly of the thicker man, until finally Ham was slowed and hurt, and tried to keep his body turned slightly sidewards. Taylor had him and moved to finish it.

Ham fired that cocked right fist.

Taylor heard the roar, glimpsed the brilliant colours, felt his body instinctively doubling over and staggering away, and through the gloom and mist saw the powerful chest and shoulders looming up and measuring him. In a desperate instinctive move, Taylor sprang sideways and young Durant missed completely.

Taylor forced his body half upright, bit his lip in concentration and through the fog saw the cheek, the ear and jaw as they moved into focus. He struck with everything he had left, aiming somewhere between jaw and temple. The blow was so solid pain exploded all the way up his arm to the shoulder.

Oaken Hamilton Durant reacted as though he had been struck from behind by an iron maul. He dropped to all fours, head hanging, dimly conscious that he could not remain like that so he tried to weave left and right. He looked exactly like a gut-shot bear; was even acting like one.

Taylor's vision was clouding up again, but he had seen his adversary, knew where he was, and by forcing himself to hold back the blackness for another moment, was able to amble over, lean to lift Ham Durant's face for a final strike, and fell across the younger man.

The added weight collapsed Durant. He fell flat on his belly in the grass, with Taylor Hawkin sprawled atop him.

A dozen yards away the bay horse stood in hock-high grass solemnly eyeing the pair of two-legged things, otherwise there was nothing to see what had happened, not even an owl or a coyote.

Chapter Eight

THE HOSTAGE

When Taylor was able to roll off the younger man and drop over onto his face in the damp grass, cold dew facilitated his return to full, but fuzzy, consciousness.

He could see the dark mound low in the grass where Hamilton Durant was lying.

For a few moments he did not move. If that grass had been a little less wet he would have been content to lie like that for an hour or two. The clamminess roused him into a sitting posture after a while. He felt the side of his head, uncertain about where exactly he had been struck, but perfectly willing to concede that Ham Durant could hit as hard as an army mule could kick.

With clearing vision, a headache, and a set of sore muscles in his neck and shoulders, Taylor felt his face and neck, looked for his hat in the grass, retrieved it and after gently dropping it upon the back of his head, pushed himself upright and hung there, momentarily allowing diminishing spirals of dizziness to subside.

Ham Durant lacked skill, but for that lack he had more than enough power to offset the lack.

Taylor looked for the gun Ham had dropped and did not find it. Even in daylight in all that tangled tall grass he probably would have been unable to find it.

He rolled a cigarette, no longer worried about the scent bringing enemies down upon him, lit up, blew smoke at the serene high sky, and when Hamilton Durant groaned, Taylor stepped over closer and leaned to look.

The younger man reached forward with bent fingers, feeling his turf. Taylor caught hold of shoulder-cloth and rocked solidly back until he had levered the heavier man into a sitting position, then he let go and stepped back a yard.

'How do you feel?' he asked, and got no answer.

Young Durant raised a hand gingerly to his swollen left cheek and jaw, moved his mouth open and closed, gently turned his head from side to side, worked his jaws a little more then looked upwards.

'What'd you hit me with?' he muttered.

Taylor offered his cigarette. Durant said, 'Don't use tobacco,' and continued to probe his sore cheek and jaw.

The bay horse was eating through the bit, which was not a good thing but Taylor did nothing about it for the time being.

When he'd finished his cigarette and dropped it in the wet tall grass Taylor said, 'Last night when the dogs barked you didn't send anyone to investigate until this morning. Tonight when they barked the whole passel of you boiled out in a man-hunt: what's the difference?'

Hamilton answered curtly. 'Last night there wasn't no reason. Tonight there is.' He eyed Taylor. 'Who are you? Mister, if you're who I think you are — gawd help you!'

'I expect He already did help me, a little bit,' stated Taylor. 'I'll give you a hand up; that grass is plumb wet.'

Hamilton accepted after making one attempt to arise unaided, and afterwards he looked for his hat, found it and also looked for his gun, but probably because he did not think he would be allowed to retrieve it even if he found the gun, he did not look for it very diligently.

He faced Taylor with an unpleasant expression. 'If you're that lawman who killed Bart up on the mesa . . .'

'What makes you think that?' asked Taylor, more interested than curious.

'You're no damned common cowboy,' answered young Durant, 'and you're plenty *coyote* about skulkin' around in the night, so my guess, mister, is that you're either a renegade or a lawman, and down here we sort of figure one isn't much different from the other.'

'Especially if you happen to be related to one of them,' said Taylor. 'Where did you leave your horse?'

Hamilton jutted his jaw. 'Yonder, out through the trees on the southward road . . . You talking about Bart?'

'No, I'm talking about your horse.' Taylor gestured. 'Walk ahead of me, Ham. Walk back to your horse and don't be smart. I'm armed and you're not. Next time I won't use my hands.'

Young Durant stared. 'By gawd you *are* that feller, aren't you?'

Taylor pointed. 'Head on out and save the questions until later.'

Taylor picked up the reins of his bay as they walked past. The animal had been eating steadily since he had first arrived in this place and whatever else he thought as he was realigned with his master, it had nothing to do with food.

Hamilton knew every yard of the pastureland they walked over and when he started into the dark trees and Taylor growled about that, Hamilton veered away without a word, skirted the trees instead of going among them, and came to a large tethered sorrel gelding whose interest was not in the men at all, his interest was in the quiet bay horse.

By this time Ham Durant had begun to consider his personal plight. When Taylor ordered him to free his horse and mount up, Durant looked over a shoulder to ask a question.

'Where we going?'

Taylor did not have a clear answer to that question even for himself, let alone for his hostage. All he knew at this juncture was that he had one, so all he said was, 'Southward, I reckon.'

'They'll get you down there,' stated Ham, snugging his cinch before stepping across saddle leather. 'They'll get you no matter which direction we ride.'

Taylor did not argue this but he was puzzled about something else. 'Why didn't you loose the dogs?'

They rode towards the dim dirt roadway as young Durant replied. 'No need, as long as you stayed in the canyon. We know every blessed inch of it for half a hundred miles on southward, and crossways as well. Besides, I don't like to run the hounds in the night. Twice I've lost good dogs to bears doing that.' He looked at Taylor. 'You never told me what you hit me with.'

'My magic wand,' stated Taylor Hawkin. 'Is there a way across this canyon and up out of here on the west side?'

'The *west side?* What in the hell ever give you an idea like that? There is nothing up there, but rocks and prickly pears and — sure there are trails, but you can't go up them unless you're a goat.'

'Then we're going to pretend we're goats,' Taylor retorted, 'because I don't like the odds trying to get out of here back up towards Holt. Not with all your brothers loose over in that direction.'

'It's not going to make a darned bit of difference,' exclaimed Ham Durant. 'East, west, north or south, you're not going up out of here, mister, and I don't care how clever you are.' He raised a thick arm, southward. 'The Croslys are down there. One of my cousins went down there this evening after he came back from Holt and told us what he'd seen up there — Bart shot to death in Holt. By now the Croslys will be stirred up too.' Ham dropped his arm. 'When my brothers figure I'm gone they'll guess how it happened, and mister, we know every high place for miles around to climb atop and keep watch from. Sooner or later they're going to see us heading west.'

'All right,' Taylor admitted. 'They'll see us. And we'll be a long way out ahead of them.'

'Naw,' said Ham, and smiled broadly. 'That's my point, lawman: we got kinsmen living over along the west barranca, too. Five housefuls of 'em. All my brothers have got to do is what my grandpaw and Old Man Crosly used to do when one or the other of them smelled In'ians — signal with the mirrors. That's how we've kept things private down in our canyon all these years. Marshal . . . ?"

'Yeah.'

'You're boxed in.'

'Maybe; but I've got a way out.'

'Yeah?'

'Yeah. You, Ham.'

As they rode, young Durant studied his captor. He was uncertain and he had a right to be, but he was not totally defeated, not as long as his brothers were out searching, and not as long as he and his captor continued to ride down Faro Canyon. Time was on the side of Ham Durant.

It troubled him though, that his captor did not seem upset nor especially worried.

When he said, 'You want some advice?' and Taylor shook his head, it bothered the younger man. All he knew about the man he was riding with was what he had heard from his cousin: this was a federal deputy marshal, and he was deadly with a Colt. That was all his cousin had said, beyond stating that Bart had been shot to death by this man.

'Why did you kill my cousin?' he asked, and got a look from Taylor Hawkin as though he didn't deserve an answer.

'I shot that bastard, Ham, because I was in the livery-barn with the liveryman and your cousin walked up behind us, and when I turned, he started to draw on me. That's the whole story and it's the plain truth.'

'And now you're trying to run,' jeered the younger man.

'No, damn it, I'm not trying to run. I'm simply trying to get at least one good hostage. I would have preferred your sister, she's much prettier, but I'll settle for you.'

'Good thing you didn't get her, they'd have killed you on sight. Anyway, like I told you — you're not going out of the canyon.'

'Not with you in front of me?'

'No. Wait until sun-up and they guess about what's happened and really turn on a manhunt, you'll find out!'

Taylor, with no immediate evident alternative, said, 'All right, I'll wait.' Then he said, 'Did you know your cousin was an outlaw?'

'Outlaw!' snorted the burly younger man. 'Can you prove it?'

Taylor looked into the round, bronzed face of the younger man. 'I can prove it.'

'Not down here you can't,' stated Ham. 'I don't give a damn if you got papers to stack to the ceiling, folks down here knew Bart, and they set no store by what a feller like you would say against him.'

Taylor continued to look into the younger man's face. 'I thought it might be like that,' he murmured. 'I've seen shut-away people like you before, Ham. Ignorant, suspicious, sceptical, against everybody and everything.'

'Ignorant! By gawd lawman, it's a good thing you got the gun!'

They continued southward until Taylor saw a branch-off which seemed to go out through a big stand of trees towards the west. He started to rein over that new trace but young Durant said, 'You won't even last until sunrise, Marshal. That's the cut-off to one of the Crosly places. You'll ride right into their yard and I'll tell 'em who you are, and they'll have you hangin' in a fir tree before breakfast.'

Taylor drew rein. 'Why warn me, then?'

'I want *us* to gather you in, not the Croslys. That's all.' Ham considered his horse's ears for a moment before also saying, 'Who saw Bart try to shoot you?'

Taylor blinked. He wasn't exactly tired yet, but it required a nimble wit to keep up with the way Ham Durant's thoughts jumped from topic to topic, and so far Taylor hadn't done too well.

'The liveryman. Feller named —'

'I know what his name is better than you do, Marshal. I've known Peter Wintering since I was up to his knee. Who else saw the gunfight?'

'No one. I told you, we were standing in his barn when your cousin walked up behind us and made his play for trouble. Ham, it was perfectly fair.'

'But that won't change much, Marshal, not when you killed a Durant.'

'I was supposed to stand there and let him shoot me?' Taylor turned back to the main roadway and they continued southward for almost a mile before Taylor thought he heard riders behind them up through the late night, and turned with a hiss for his prisoner to follow, and rode off into a thicket of trees and underbrush.

It was one rider, not a party of them, and

he had indeed been behind them, but he wasn't tracking them, even if that had been possible in the darkness, because he was riding too fast and wasn't looking in any direction but directly ahead.

Taylor dryly said, 'Paul Revere,' and young Durant answered tartly, 'You'll wish it was by morning. That's Job. He was Bart's brother. If he'd caught you, Marshal, you'd have died sitting your saddle.'

Taylor sighed. According to Ham all they had down here was deadly, unreasoning people.

They did not return to the roadway but rode eastward over across a wide, rolling meadow. They didn't encounter the creek until Taylor was almost of the opinion that they were not going to, then the ground turned unsteady underfoot and dead ahead a dozen or so yards they ploughed on across it again, but down here the grass was so thick and tangled the creek did not have a watercourse, it was rather spread out for almost a hundred yards through the reeds and grass and ripgut-stalks.

Ham acted disgusted. 'What's the sense of doing this?' he demanded.

Taylor eyed him. For a prisoner Ham was unusually bold.

By the time the footing firmed up again

their horses had black swamp-mud to their knees, and because moving through sucking, clammy, evil-smelling earth like that was hard on the animals, when they finally were back on solid footing again they wanted to halt and rest. Taylor allowed it, looped his reins and manufactured a cigarette under Ham Durant's disapproving scowl. When he lit up and exhaled at the slanting moon, young Durant said, 'That's another thing; if Mother Nature had meant for you to smoke she'd have stuck a chimney atop your head.'

Taylor was unperturbed. His estimate had them about six miles southward from the Durant ranch-yard, and perhaps a mile and a half eastward, over across the creek in the direction of the far barranca, but all they could see from here was a stand of trees beyond them, between them and the barranca.

'Any trails up to Holt from down here?' he asked mildly.

'The road is northward six, seven miles and by now you'd ought to know that,' stated the younger man.

'I know where the road is. What I asked you was: are there any trails up to the mesa from this far south . . . Ham? Remember now; we were raised to hate a liar.'

Young Durant hung his head in thought for a long while, wrestling with his conscience, and finally he said, 'What difference would it make even if you got up there — they are still going to get you.'

Taylor was untouched. 'Are there any trails — Ham?'

'Yes, damn it, there's a trail. The Croslys made it before I was born. But they are going to catch us before we can get up it, and even if they don't, if they don't catch us until we reach Holt, you are still a goner.'

Taylor sighed. 'Head for the Croslys' trail. Be quiet about it. And don't go through those trees over yonder . . . Ham?'

'Yeah.'

'I have no intention at all of hurting you. I'm not going to feel right about it if you force me to change that.'

Hamilton wore a wry look as he turned to ride off in the lead.

The night was steadily advancing, the chill was increasing as the hours passed, and visibility became worse instead of better, but Ham Durant did not try to escape. He did not in fact even try to lead them through one of the forest-stands they encountered along the way. He left Taylor Hawkin thinking that he was too confident of the outcome of his abduction to want to run risks now.

Chapter Nine

TO THE MESA

Taylor was not happy. He had wanted a hostage, but that hadn't been his sole reason for descending to Faro Canyon, and in fact he'd have been just as pleased to have been able to talk to Barbara for a short while, and return up out of the canyon without a hostage.

There were never any guarantees in this life. The way things had worked out he hadn't spoken to the handsome girl, and he had her truculent, talkative, almost obnoxious brother as his prisoner — and he still was not out of Faro Canyon.

Also, as Hamilton had told him, there were a lot of Durants somewhere over on the east side of the canyon between Taylor Hawkin and the road up to the mesa-top.

They rode for about a mile in total silence. It seemed to be darker over closer to the eastern canyon wall, and it also seemed to be colder, but that could have been Taylor's imagination.

He began to expect trouble, at least to

begin to think in terms of it the closer he got to the east side even though they were at least five miles southward of the road, and were probably closer to six miles southward of where he thought most of the Durants might be.

The first inkling he had that they might get out of Faro Canyon without trouble was when his guide halted in a starlighted dry clearing and pointed. 'That's the old Crosly trace,' Ham explained, pointing to a surprisingly good uphill roadway. It at one time would have accommodated wagons — one at a time — but since falling into disuse it would no longer do that, but it would accommodate a pair of riders abreast and the grade was actually as good or perhaps even slightly better than the gradient of the Durant-road, northward.

Ham turned. 'Want to risk it?'

Taylor saw no risk. 'Does that road worry you? If it does you'd have had heart failure on some of the trails through the mountains I used tracking your cousin down here from Denver.' He gestured. 'Go on up. I'll follow.'

'They're going to see us,' stated Ham. 'We'll be pinned against the side of this darned —'

'Damn it, ride on up and be quiet!'

96

Ham obeyed but not until he had made one final statement. 'By now my brothers are atop the mesa. They'll come down this far; they know where the old Crosly road is.'

Taylor did not speak. His bay was getting leg-weary and finally, he was beginning to feel wrung-out too.

They startled a deer a third of the way up. It dived over the edge and they could hear its clattering descent down towards the canyon floor.

The view of Faro Canyon from half way up, in moonlight and starshine, was ghostly. It was, Taylor told himself, like being suspended in space and time looking back down into the world a man had recently left behind, and also being able to look out over whatever came next, a different kind of eerie world.

He came back to reality with a wrench when up ahead a few yards his guide stopped dead-still in the middle of the trail, looking upwards. Ham turned and fiercely gestured for silence.

Instantly, Taylor halted, stepped down and lay a hand lightly across the nostrils of the bay. He wasn't sure what Ham had heard but if it were riders up there, Taylor did not want his bay to scent them and nicker.

For a while Ham stood beside his sorrel with one arm upraised, his head tilted to indicate that he was looking upwards as well as listening. Finally, he dropped his arm and sighed audibly.

Without a word he swung back across the saddle and urged his sorrel forward. Taylor rode up close and hissed at him.

'What was it?'

Ham answered without turning. 'At least one rider, but maybe two or three I couldn't tell. I was scairt they might turn off and start down.'

Taylor scratched. '*You* were scairt!'

Ham did not speak again, but for the balance of the ride to the mesa-top he kept his head tilted.

Nothing happened. If those riders were patrolling they must have continued southward a long distance before turning back. In any event Taylor and his hostage reached the mesa, turned off up there, paused to look and listen and to blow their horses, and Ham suddenly said, 'You figure I was tryin' to keep those brothers of mine from coming down there and getting you? Like hell; I was between them and you. *That's* why I was helpful back there.'

Taylor accepted this. 'You have good hearing, Ham,' he said.

'Which way from here?'

'Holt.'

'Town? You want to head for town?'

Taylor cocked an eye. 'You said we couldn't possibly get up out of your canyon. We got out. You said your kinsmen were boiling all over this part of the area. All we heard was a rider or two and they might not even have been anyone you knew. Ham; maybe it's just luck, but I don't think the disasters you keep predicting are going to happen. Now head out, will you?'

'You'll find out,' said the burly younger man, and now that they could ride side by side again, he slouched along for a while before starting up a conversation again. 'Who says my cousin broke the law up in Colorado?'

Taylor looked around. 'He robbed a bank in Denver, shot and killed the banker when he tried to stop your cousin, and a woman cashier was standing near the door. He shot and killed her too. I've got the full statement in my pocket plus my orders from the U.S. Marshal in Cheyenne, but it's too dark for you to read them. There is also a newspaper account, which I don't have with me, in which four witnesses give their stories.'

'Lousy lies.'

'Come on, Ham, damn it all, they aren't

all lousy lies and I think you realize it.' Taylor studied the oaken man's blunt, square profile. 'Ham?'

'Yeah.'

'You knew what your cousin was.'

Durant rode in strong silence.

'If your brothers and other kinsmen aren't blind and dumb and deaf they'd know too . . . And Barbara; she knew. She knew I'd ridden through and she knew Bart had gone ahead. She was supposed to pass word to him if a stranger came into the canyon. She didn't send him word.'

The younger man looked quizzical. 'What does that mean? Maybe no one rode up to Holt yesterday.'

'Clanny folks look out for their own,' stated Taylor. 'If it had been you or maybe your brothers, you'd have seen to it that Bart was warned. If Barbara didn't do that, I'd say she had a reason. There's got to be someone down in Faro Canyon who's not against the law.'

'We're not against the law,' growled the younger man. 'But I don't expect very many of us are going to take the word of the first stranger who rides through. Since my family started out in the canyon, we've seen a lot of trouble, and we've had reason to be suspicious.'

Taylor did not argue with the Durant philosophy, he fitted it to his predicament. 'You've got reason to be suspicious now,' he said to the younger man, 'but only until you've heard the facts, had them proved to you. After that, protecting an outlaw makes you just as bad.'

'Well,' stated Ham dryly, 'it's darned clear that none of us protected him, isn't it? He's dead, isn't he, and if me and my brothers had ridden up here yesterday to protect him, *he* wouldn't be dead today, *you* would.'

'Are you telling me those kinsmen of yours won't be around, come morning?'

'No,' stated Hamilton Durant. 'Not by a darned sight. They'll be around and so most likely will a herd more of the folks from down below. I been warning you about that all night, but you'll have your chance.'

To Taylor's way of thinking there appeared to be some strong doubts on that score; none of the men he had spoken to in Holt had given him the chance of a snowball in hell.

Somewhere between the two views he thought his solution might appear — as long as he kept a hostage. It was a case of listening to everyone, then making an independent decision and acting upon it.

'There is to be a hearing,' he said, and young Durant snorted.

'When the Durants and the Croslys ride up and set in the firehouse where they hold those hearings, there's hardly a seat left for anyone else. You can guess how those hearings go.' Durant stood in his stirrups. 'Town's up ahead, Marshal. Did you figure you'd just ride in and get Frank Beckman to lock me up for you?'

'No, I figured to take care of looking after you by myself, and I didn't figure on telling Beckman at all.' Taylor angled his horse a little and jerked his head for his captive to follow.

Chapter Ten

END OF A LONG NIGHT

For a while as they rode along young Durant was quiet and thoughtful, then, as they got within sight of the half dozen lights up ahead where the town was, he said, 'I'll tell you something, Marshal, that might interest you. When my sister came back home after sharing fry-bread with you, she came out back where I was, with my hounds, and we talked for a spell.'

Taylor was interested. 'She told you she'd found the lawman who was after Bart?'

'Well, she never said you were the lawman. She said maybe it was a coincidence, you arriving over the north rims down into the canyon right at this time. Maybe you were just a cowboy riding through.'

Young Durant glanced over at Hawkin in the bad light. 'She's pretty isn't she?' he said suddenly.

Taylor nodded. 'Prettiest woman I ever saw.'

'Yeah, well; she had herself convinced before she got back home after talkin' with you, that regardless of what Bart had said, she wasn't going to slip up to Holt on the mesa, find him and tip your hand to him so's he could gun you down, too.'

'She told you that, Ham?'

'Not exactly, Marshal.' Durant shrugged. 'She's been my sister since she was right small. We been close friends for about that long too, and that's different than being kin-folk. I know Barb I expect as well as her maw knows her, and a lot better than my brothers know her. Mostly, they like her, but she's a girl.'

'Yeah,' stated Taylor dryly, 'for a fact she's a girl.'

They rode into the lower end of Holt, down where the livery-barn was, but below it, down where a few tarpaper shacks had been erected by people too poor or too lazy to take teams to the sidehills and snake back logs to make respectable residences.

'I'm goin' to help you,' said Ham Durant without looking at Taylor Hawkin. 'Not for your sake, mind. For *her* sake. She thought you were a gentleman. She told me that.' Ham looked at Taylor. 'I don't see how she came to the notion; you look like any other rangeman to me.'

'Thanks,' Taylor said, ironically.

Durant looked sharply at Taylor. 'You being sarcastic again? If you are you'd better believe it when I tell you there isn't a soul around who's going to need help more'n you.'

Ham reined over to the east side of the roadway and when they came abreast of a dark little crooked alleyway he turned in, jerking his head for Taylor to follow. Taylor did, and at the same time he loosened the Colt he was wearing.

But Ham did not look back nor make any threatening move. He led the way up through the narrow, cluttered alleyway until Taylor guessed they were roughly in the area behind Preston Lynch's saloon, then Hamilton reined to a halt, swung off and said, 'Come along. Mind your step; folks never haul trash away, they pitch it out here.'

He led the way to a ramshackle old carriage house made of logs which even by starshine looked to have been constructed as a fortification rather than someone's elaborate outbuilding.

Inside, it was as dark as the inside of a well except for the west wall which had a big glassless window in it, and someone's lamp burning over across the alleyway shone in, not with a whole lot of light but with enough for Taylor to see the horse-stalls along the west wall.

Without commenting Hamilton Durant went to work off-saddling. He moved briskly and said nothing until he was ready to lift down the saddle, then he leaned and looked at Taylor. 'This place belongs to my paw. Once, years back, he had the stage and mail franchise. That was before I was born. Go ahead and off-saddle, Marshal, we can catch some sleep before breakfast time.' Ham's teeth shone in a wide smile. 'Don't worry, I'm not going to swarm over and take that pistol off you.' Durant continued to stand and watch as Taylor made no immediate move to off-saddle. 'Marshal,' he eventually said, on a note of protest. 'I told you — I'm going to help you.'

'Yeah,' retorted Taylor in the ghostly reflected light. 'That's what that little feller named Howard said to Jesse James.'

Ham's faintly-seen face assumed an expression of unmistakable disgust. 'You don't believe me,' he groaned. 'I been riding all over hell with you tonight, lookin' you over and takin' my time arrivin' at this decision for my sister's sake.' Ham stepped around the broad rump of his horse. 'Look,' he said, and hoisted a booted thick leg to a broken old keg, pulled up the leg of his trouser until a cowhide boot-top was exposed, and palmed the little under-and-over derringer .44 in the boot-holster there. He pointed it at Taylor, held it like that a silent moment, then returned it to the boot-top holster and dropped his trouser-leg as he straightened back. 'You think, coming up out of Faro Canyon I couldn't have used that on you? Or back when we were ridin' the south road down there and I was a few feet behind you?'

Taylor sighed, leaned to loosen the cinch of his horse and said, 'You sure didn't look the type to me. That's a renegade trick.'

'Or a hunter,' retorted the younger man. 'Lots of times I got to climb over a mile of boulders to get to a bear or cougar my dogs put to earth, and lugging a darned awkward carbine or packing along ten pounds of Colt and bulletbelt don't much appeal to me.' Ham lifted down his saddle, finally, bumped his horse's rump so the animal would walk into one of the stalls, and lugged his saddle to a swinging long pole where he heaved it across, then leaned on it looking back.

'How old are you, Marshal?'

Taylor frowned. 'What the hell's that got to do with anything?'

'My sister is twenty-three.'

Taylor looked across saddle-leather. 'I'm thirty-eight.'

'Well, it's a mite agey,' murmured the burly younger man, and lifted off his hat to run bent fingers through that mane of taffy hair before resettling the hat. Then he shrugged. 'Well, it's her choice, not mine.'

Taylor continued to lean and stare. 'What's her choice?'

'Keepin' you for a pet,' said Ham Durant, and briskly swarmed up a loft-ladder. 'Put your horse in the stall next to mine and that way I'll know where to pitch down the hay. It's darker'n the depths of hell up here.'

Taylor slung his outfit from the saddle-pole, led the bay into its designated stall, then looked up as Ham Durant flung hay down from the loft. As though in response to Taylor's thought, Ham called from overhead.

'We always keep a little jag of hay up here, for when some of us come to Holt and figure to spend the night here.'

The loft-ladder was a fir log with notched-in short cross-pieces nailed to it and the way hefty Ham Durant came swarming down it made Taylor Hawkin wince. The log wasn't that strong nor that sound, it seemed to noticeably bend and groan under the burly man's descending weight.

Taylor's opinion of his hostage had been in process of formulation all night, and he still thought Ham Durant was needlessly talkative, and under some circumstances unless Ham's behaviour changed, he would also be obnoxious. But clearly there were other facets to Ham's personality and character Taylor had not reached yet. One of them had been revealed just as they were entering the sleeping town: Ham Durant's fondness for his sister was encouraging him to do something Taylor Hawkin knew very well Ham was going to have occasion to regret later on. But Taylor needed an ally, there was no question about that, and if he could acquire one from among the Durants of Faro Canyon — after having killed a Durant — he would certainly offer no objection.

But when they were standing together in the chill after the horses had been cared for, Taylor spoke out frankly by saying, 'It's not like Bart was a Crosly, Ham. I don't know your family at all, except Barbara, but from what folks been telling me up here on the mesa, the Durants will hang me on sight. I don't figure you'd ought to voluntarily buy in. I'll be out of here one way or another in a day or two, but you've got to live here for maybe another forty years.'

Ham's answer was blunt. 'You'll be out of here in a day or two all right. Alone, Marshal, you aren't going to see sundown.'

Taylor did not believe it was that bad, even though everyone else clearly thought so, and his reason was simply that because he had been able to escape from Faro Canyon and return to the mesa-top where there was a degree of resentment against the people from down below, if he had not exactly returned to the territory of his friends, he had at least got back among the people like Pres Lynch and Pete Wintering who were at the very least, slightly antagonistic towards the men from Faro Canyon.

Maybe he was relying upon something which would melt away in a crisis, but he did not believe so. He had been making independent judgements of men for a long time. Maybe he was wrong this time but until the proof was before him he wouldn't yield to doubt.

'You wouldn't throw down on your own brothers,' he told young Durant. 'Listen to me; go on back. I'll forget that business about needin' a hostage. Up here I don't need one anyway. Go on back and —'

'Let me tell you something, Marshal,'

stated Durant, interrupting with a gesture. 'I got rattler-bit three years ago. You know who looked after me. Not just my maw and a couple of my aunts — who gave me hell for lettin' a snake get that close — but my sister. She never blamed me, never even *looked* like I'd been careless, and she'd get to laughin' with me sometimes . . . Naw; I'll stay here with you.'

'Ham,' exclaimed Taylor Hawkin, 'I only talked to your sister once. For maybe fifteen minutes, and she wasn't real friendly then, either. You know what I think? You're a nosy damned would-be match-maker. I'll make a bet your sister's no more interested in me than . . . how in hell could she be? We ate some fry-bread and she made me feel like I was an intruder. She doesn't know me from Adam's off ox. For all she knows I could be as bad as your cousin was.'

Hamilton weathered all this without changing expression, then he yawned. 'I'm tired,' he drawled, turned on his heel and crossed into the shadows.

There were some bunks with rope springs in another part of the old log carriage-house, or way-station or whatever it had been, but they did not go in search of them.

Ham set the example by kicking up some dusty old hay and draping his smelly saddleblanket over it, then dropping wearily down. As he rolled up onto his side he said, 'If that gun of mine is lost down there in the damned mud and grass, you owe me for one, Marshal.'

Then he started to snore.

Along with several other traits which Taylor Hawkin nearly resented was this ability of the burly younger man to fall asleep anywhere, under almost any circumstances.

Taylor checked their horses, found the animals entirely comfortable, and went in search of his own bed of dusty hay. He did not possess Ham Durant's ability to roll over, close his eyes and instantly go to sleep. He was not just older with a more fully developed conscience — one of the inevitables of being older — but he also had peril on all sides of him.

None the less he slept, and when something hairy walked across his face he did not know it. He did not in fact know anything for a short while. He was tired to the bone.

Dawn came later than usual for this time of year. The reason was visible off across the eastern sky, low down, where a wide, grey-black cloud hovered menacingly. The sun arose early but its light could not penetrate that distant rain-cloud.

The air had a metallic taste. Taylor

opened his eyes, wrinkled his nose, waited a moment then sat up looking around.

Ham was lying there, thick arms raised, hands clasped beneath his head, gazing steadily upwards. He rolled his head. 'Goin' to rain,' he announced, settling for Taylor the question which had prompted him to sit up. 'But not until this afternoon or evening.'

Ham sighed loudly then sat up, brushed off hay and spat aside. 'By now they're boilin' around down there like hornets in a stick-hit hive.' He grinned at Taylor and rubbed a ham-sized hand over his stubbly jaw. 'Job'll be mad as hell. Job's my brother — next oldest above me. He'll be fit to be tied.'

Taylor nodded. 'I can understand that. You've been missing all night.'

'Naw,' grumbled Ham, getting up to his feet and shaking like a dog coming out of a creek. 'Not because I've disappeared. Job'll be fit to be tied because he'll have to feed my hounds.' Ham tried to reach around to knock off the few stubbornly adhering stalks of straw. 'Job doesn't like hunting dogs. In fact he don't like hunting. You known very many like that?'

Taylor hadn't. 'No, not very many,' he muttered, as he rolled up to his feet. He too shook off the hay, but because he was never very loquacious first thing in the morning, he allowed Ham to make what conversation they had, and when his retorts dwindled off into monosyllabic grunts, Ham eventually perceived their difference in this regard, and became quiet for the length of time that was required for them to feed and water their horses, and to then cuff their salty backs with a set of currycombs and brushes someone had abandoned years earlier in a box nailed to a side of the wall.

With that chore taken care of Ham said, 'Marshal; I'm a man as need food.'

Taylor, gazing at the thick, somewhat massive body in front or him, nodded. 'Lead off.' At the door of their log hideout he also said, 'Ham; it's going to jar hell out of folks on the mesa if we go to the cafe side by side.'

Ham was unperturbed by this possibility. 'Let 'em be jarred then, eh?'

Taylor said no more. Another aspect of the Durant character was clearly an unalterable stubbornness once a Durant had decided upon his course of behaviour.

When they crossed the alley, struck out single-file up through a dog-trot between two store buildings and emerged out front upon the scuffed plankwalk of Main Street,

Taylor had a question for his burly companion.

'Is Barbara pig-headed too?'

Ham looked surprised, then he slowly looked amused, and finally he laughed, 'No, but then Barb's more like the Croslys. They're a tough breed of people, Marshal, but different. I mean, they won't come rushing up here all fired up and making war-medicine. My maw is a Crosly. That makes Barb a half-Crosly, don't it?'

'And you too,' said Taylor, stepping to the doorway of the cafe to hold it for Ham to enter first.

Inside, Pete Wintering and his dayman were at breakfast over along the counter. So were six or seven other early-feeding townsmen. They looked up . . . looked up again more slowly the second time, and unabashedly stared.

The victim of a grisly death at the hands of the Faro Canyon Durants had just walked in for breakfast, with a Durant!

Chapter Eleven

A SURPRISE

Pres Lynch squinted at Wintering. 'If you say so I believe it, but —'

'That darned Hamilton always was a sort of maverick,' grumbled the liveryman. 'Hell; when I seen that empty horse-stall last night I'd have bet ten dollars gold that federal lawman had high-tailed it. In fact me and the nightman said that exact thing: he's gone on the run, and good riddance, because now I won't have to testify at the coroner's hearing.'

Pres scowled. 'You'd have to testify anyway. It wouldn't make any difference whether the lawman was here or not. I helped Frank get up the summonses this morning before sun-up. You'll be served with one.' At Wintering's look his friend spread both hands wide.

'That son of a bitch was a Durant. If he'd been a stranger passing through or maybe a cowboy lookin' for work and nobody'd known him, we wouldn't have needed a coroner's inquest. But he was a Durant.'

'Lousy robber and murderer,' said Wintering.

'Maybe so, but there's still got to be a hearing . . . What the hell is Ham up to, partnering with the man who shot his cousin?'

'Maybe he's going to pin a medal on him,' said the liveryman, whose disposition required the shoring up of much coffee every morning before it improved any. 'Pres, ever since Bart was first making trouble around this part of the territory, we all figured he'd end up on a gallows somewhere.'

'You never said that out loud, though,' stated the saloonman. 'You care for some Irish coffee?'

Wintering's disgruntled expression brightened slightly. 'You got some?'

Wordlessly, Pres went to his back room, brought out a coffeepot, filled two cups, poured in a liberal lacing of rye whisky, and set one cup before the liveryman. Now, finally, Pete Wintering's demeanour began to permanently change for the better. He even smiled as he hoisted the cup and inhaled the aroma.

'Well,' stated the liveryman, 'it's done. I'm not afraid to testify. I'd just as soon I didn't have to, but I'm not going to weasel out neither . . . Say, this is fine coffee, Pres. I didn't know you could make decent coffee.'

'You've drunk coffee in here before,' stated the saloonman.

Wintering agreed. 'Yeah. Lots of times, but like I said, I didn't know you could make decent coffee.'

Pres's scarred, lined, weathered countenance closed down a little towards his friend. 'Maybe they'll shoot you right during the hearing,' he said, sounding hopeful. 'Naw; they'll wait until you come outside to do it.'

Frank Beckman walked in. It was early, only a short while after breakfast-time, so the saloon had no customers yet, and both the coffee-drinkers turned in frank curiosity to see who the newcomer was. When they recognized the constable, they returned to their coffee without a greeting or a word until Beckman strolled over and said, ' 'Morning, gents,' then they both dutifully nodded and muttered a greeting in return.

'Missed you at the cafe bright and early this morning.' said the liveryman, rolling his eyes around to Pres Lynch as he spoke.

'Slept in,' stated the lawman, leaning. 'Pres, you got another cup of that Irish coffee?'

'You should have been down there,' said

Wintering. 'That federal marshal who shot Bart Durant was there.'

Frank slowly shifted his weight and twisted to look. 'This morning? You sure, Pete?'

'Sure as I am that I'm standing here this minute, Frank.'

'I thought he'd left the country. Your nightman came up before I locked up the jailhouse last night and said he'd ridden out.'

'He had,' conceded Wintering, deliberately drawing this out because while he did not exactly *dis*like Constable Beckman, he was not his close friend either, but Pete probably would have done this to anyone; he was one of those people who dearly enjoyed jarring the hell out of someone. 'Yeah, Frank, he rode out last night. Only he come back, and when he came into the cafe for breakfast this morning . . .'

Wintering hesitated. He and Pres Lynch were watching Beckman's face now.

'When he come in for breakfast this morning, Frank, he had Hamilton Durant with him. And Ham's hip-holster didn't have no gun in it. You know what some of us at the counter figured, after they had ate and walked out? We figured by gawd that federal lawman went down into the canyon

119

last night and somehow or other baited Ham out and away from the ranch, and taken him hostage, and brought him up here to make damned certain no Durants'll show up in Holt today for the hearing, with cocked guns in their hands.'

Frank Beckman remained twisted from the waist for a long while staring at Wintering before he slowly straightened around and glared at the saloonman. 'Where's that coffee I asked for five minutes ago?' he irately demanded, and Lynch went at once to his back room to get it.

During his absence Wintering leaned, sipped coffee, and enjoyed the consternation he had caused. 'Frank; you'd better find those two and rescue Ham,' he said. 'If Job and all them others get up here and you haven't rescued —'

'Damn you,' snarled the angry and upset lawman. 'I've said it before: if you'd just mind your own darned business, that livery-barn would do twice as much business as it does.' He turned on his heel and stamped out of the saloon.

Pres returned with the Irish coffee, set it atop the bar and looked left and right.

Wintering appropriated the coffee, shoved his own empty cup away and leaned closer to the bar as he sipped his second cup. His mood continued to brighten as the moments passed.

'He left,' the liveryman said to the saloonman. 'I figure we put it on him a mite heavy. He's one of those fellers who can't stand much first thing in the morning. Pity, isn't it?'

Pres looked sceptically at his friend. 'Yeah, it's a real pity. Of course you aren't like that.'

Pete cocked a good-natured bright eye. 'Me? You know a darned sight better. Me, I got an even disposition. This morning for example . . .'

'This morning, Pete, you're gettin' warmed up by my rye whisky, that's what.' Lynch shrugged and reached for his cup.

It was empty. He looked down into it trying to remember; he was almost certain the cup had been half full when he'd gone out back. *Almost* certain.

Pete leaned and sipped and mellowly eyed his friend. 'You care to know what I *really* figure? I'll tell you anyway, Pres: Ham isn't no hostage of that federal lawman. Ham is *with* him. Someway or another they got to be friends. I watched 'em in the cafe. You know, Ham's as strong as a bear and he was sitting on the lawman's right side — where the lawman's holstered pistol was by gawd — and knowin' Ham like I do, I'm here to tell you he could have grabbed that gun . . . Only he didn't. He sat and ate like a horse, like he always does, and once in a while they'd speak a little, real quiet, and hell, they wasn't no more enemies than you and I are.'

Having delivered himself of this observation of priceless worth, the liveryman put down his empty coffee cup, peered sadly into it and raised soft eyes.

Without a scrap of compassion Pres grabbed the cup and dropped it into his bucket of greasy water behind the bar.

Wintering heaved a big sigh, nodded solemnly, turned, drew a steady bead upon the spindle-doors across the empty big old barn-like room, squared his shoulders and set out.

He made it unerringly and disappeared out into the newday sunlight, which had belatedly arrived, paused once more to gather himself together, shoulders up, stomach sucked in, head erect, aiming this time for the opposite side of the roadway. From over there he only had to follow the plankwalk southward to the lower end of town where his livery-barn was.

Behind him, in the saloon, Pres Lynch glanced into his empty cup again and mildly swore. He had never before seen any of the respectable men around town skunked out of their nest before eight o'clock in the morning. It disgusted him a little, but that disgust might not have been as virulent as it was if all that Irish coffee hadn't gone out of his saloon free.

He was drawn to the doorway, finally, out of plain curiosity. By the time he arrived over there Wintering had got across the empty roadway. He was now hiking with great dignity, as erect as a ramrod, past Frank Beckman's jailhouse, and he was not holding to a true course at all although he certainly thought he was. He weaved like a man walking the rolling deck of a ship.

Beckman stepped to the doorway of the jailhouse, stopped and stared. Upon the opposite side of the roadway the harness-maker came from his place of business drying both hands upon a wax-stiff brown apron. He also stopped in his doorway to look. He reached and shoved his eye-glasses up his forehead and stared harder.

A pair of motionless men down in the tree-shade of the livery-barn yard stood and watched, until one of them shifted position a little as he rolled a smoke, and said, 'I don't believe it.'

The other one, thicker and younger and

with unshorn taffy hair, was nonplussed. 'By gawd, me too. I've known him all my life and never once did I even hear anyone say he was a secret drinker. What time is it?'

Taylor finished the cigarette and lighted it before replying, his blue stare cold and thoughtful. 'Not yet nine in the morning, Ham. That damned fool is my star witness.'

'Not today he isn't,' stated young Durant. 'Look at him. Why hell, he can't hit the ground with his hat.'

Taylor inhaled, exhaled, considered the oncoming glassy-eyed liveryman a moment longer, then drifted his gaze back on up the northward roadway to where Pres Lynch was standing out front of his saloon.

'He came out of Lynch's place, Ham,' Hawkin murmured. 'Hell; I thought Lynch was on my side.'

Young Durant made a cogent observation. 'Pres never sat on his belly and poured it down him, Marshal. A man don't get skunked unless he's willing to.'

Durant scratched, eyed the rolling gait of the oncoming liveryman, and turned only when the dayman stepped forth from the front of the barn, leaned upon his manure-fork and blurted out: 'F'Chriz'sake!'

Ham was spurred by this exclamation of astonishment. 'We got to get black java down him, Marshal, until he can float out of here and testify. We got to get the darned old idiot sober.'

'I think I'll go up and talk to Lynch,' said Taylor, but the younger man raised a thick arm. 'No, by gawd; you help me with this fool.' Ham turned towards the hostler. 'You got coffee in the harness-room?'

The dayman looked at Ham with a shocked expression. 'Coffee? No; I think I drank the last of it a while ago.'

'Well, shag your butt to the pump, fill that lousy pot with fresh water and stoke up the fire,' ordered Ham Durant.

The dayman turned and fled back into the barn.

Pete Wintering left the plankwalk more by instinct than presence of mind, heading for the opening into his barn. He did not see either of the two men standing motionless in tree-shade watching him. He knew his condition, but what especially intrigued him was not that he was drunk so early in the day, what fascinated him in an abstract sort of way was how swiftly and unerringly that laced coffee had inebriated him, and how very pleasant this condition was.

He was not a hard-drinking man and although he took whisky and beer occasionally as he felt the need, he had not been actually drunk very many times in his life, and never before this early in the morning.

It was, however, a decidedly pleasant experience. As he walked past the pair of cold-eyed men in his yard, he decided that perhaps under suitable conditions he might very well try it again, some morning.

He did not hear the pair of men turn in behind him and follow him down through the runway in the direction of his harness-room, nor did he have an inkling that those two were going to ruin forever his wonderful recollections of this very unique early-morning experience, destroying his illusive notion that he might do this again, some day.

Chapter Twelve

SHOWDOWN ON THE WAY

For the constable, what Pres Lynch had to say was trouble atop trouble, and when Jake Rowan walked down from his stage-company yard to stand in Beckman's jailhouse doorway, head cocked in that quizzical way, as he said, 'They're coming up from Faro Canyon,' added the final stone to his burden.

He said, 'Who's coming, damn it?' although he knew perfectly well who Jake had referred to.

Rowan's bent head and upward glance did not alter as he patiently answered. 'The Durants, and maybe the Croslys although the feller who told me he seen 'em coming up the road didn't say anything about the Croslys. I sort of figure the Croslys will come up their old trace and cut us off to the south.'

Even Pres Lynch was annoyed by that. 'Cut us off,' he exclaimed. 'What the hell are you talking about? This isn't a war, Jake.'

Rowan snickered. 'You that sure, are you?' he asked, and backed out of the doorway to turn and head on across the road where he could add his mote to the uncertainty in town this morning.

'Ought to wring his neck,' growled Pres Lynch. 'Set it straight on his shoulders for a change.' Pres looked at Constable Beckman. 'Somebody'd better get over there to the top of the pass, hadn't they?'

'What for?' demanded the constable. 'Roll rocks down?'

'No, confound it, not to roll rocks down. To meet the Durants and palaver with them.'

Beckman was agreeable to that. 'Sure. Find Ham and send him. They aren't going to listen to anyone else. They never do, you know.'

Beckman was not as irresolute as he acted and sounded. He gathered up the papers he and the saloonman had worked on. 'I'm going to the firehouse and set up the chairs and all,' he announced. He and Lynch exchanged a look. 'Where the hell is Ham?'

Pres Lynch had no idea. 'I asked at the cafe and at the general store. They been at the old way-station out back; like I told you. I found their horses and where they slept in the hay over there.'

'Not where they *been*, but where they *are*,' muttered Constable Beckman, then as he headed for the door he allowed the restraint to slip just for a revealing moment as he said, 'I wish that damned federal deputy'd broke his leg coming down off the north-ward peaks, or had taken a fit or something afterwards . . . You know what my position is?'

Pres knew. 'Yeah. You're related to them by marriage.'

'That's only part of it, Pres. I got to oppose them and that's bad. If they make any kind of trouble that's not allowed by the law books I work by, I got to face them — what the hell chance do I have?'

Pres did not reply. He waited a moment, until Frank turned to stalk on his way across the roadway and northward to the firehouse to prepare the room for the hearing which was to convene at ten o'clock, then Pres also left the jailhouse, but he hiked southward to find Pete Wintering, shame him sober if he could, and then to get Pete to help him go up through town before the hearing con-vened, and inspire a dozen or two local townsmen to appear at the firehouse armed and willing to back up their town constable.

When he got down there and walked into the harness-room he stopped stock-still.

Ham Durant, the man he had tried to locate earlier, was patiently explaining to an ill-looking Pete Wintering that unless Pete continued drinking black coffee, he was going to straddle him while the U.S. deputy marshal and the dayman poured it down him.

Pete saw Pres Lynch by craning around, and cried to him for help. 'They're trying to kill me,' he wailed. 'I already drunk so much coffee I went out back and heaved my boot-straps, Pres. You got to get the constable down here.'

Pres crossed both arms and glared. 'If I do, Pete, he'll kick your butt up around your ears. You're the only witness he's got for the defendant — that means for the feller who is charged.' Pres jutted his jaw towards Taylor Hawkin. 'Him.'

Pres remained in that obdurate stance and shifted his glare to Ham Durant. 'He's sober. You want to scour him? If he gets sick in the firehouse . . . Ham, he don't need any more coffee.'

Taylor stepped back. He and the dayman critically studied the ashen face of the sweating liveryman. Taylor concurred with the saloonman.

'He's right, Ham. The damned fool is sober enough.'

Hamilton Durant stepped away and put down the dented tin coffee cup, eyed Wintering and turned as the saloonman said, 'Where in hell you been? We looked all over hell for you a while back.'

'What of it?' growled the younger man.

'Your folks are on their way up out of the canyon, that's what about it,' retorted Pres Lynch.

'I'd ought to punch you for getting Pete drunk this morning,' growled the young Durant, ignoring what Pres Lynch had said.

The saloonman reacted with vigour. 'Me! I didn't get the darned buzzard drunk. I gave him a little Irish coffee is all, and he hogged a troughful and got drunk without any help from me. In fact he took some of that coffee I'd fixed for Frank . . . Me? Hamilton, I never got *any*body drunk in my saloon unless they asked for it, and even then I've always made a practice of —'

'You should've been a preacher,' growled the larger man. 'Who said they're coming up from the canyon?'

'Some rangerider who was over in that area and saw 'em on the road,' replied Pres, then he and the dayman and Taylor Hawkin stood in silence gazing at the younger man.

Finally, when Ham did not speak, the dayman offered a suggestion. 'We could head south. Start out right now and we could be couple miles down the road before they even get atop the mesa.'

Pete Wintering, sitting hunched with both forearms resting on his legs at the desk, spoke without raising his hanging head. 'You don't know what you're talking about; the Croslys will be coming up *their* trace. You couldn't get — well, maybe *you* could, because no one figures you're involved in this — but none of the rest of us could get a mile down that road.' Pete lifted his grey face with an effort. 'Go on back to work,' he ordered. 'Get out of here and get to cleanin' the stalls and lookin' after the livestock, damn it all.'

The dayman turned without a word, but with an expression of enormous relief, and scuttled out of the harness-room. His absence made the small room slightly less crowded, but not a whole lot less, and otherwise nothing much had changed, Pete was still more ill than well, and troubled in the bargain. His earlier idea of perhaps making an occasional interlude of morning drinking was completely forgotten.

Preston Lynch said, 'What he needs is a big glass of warm milk.'

No one disputed this and no one offered to go around town to find a glass of milk for the liveryman either. Taylor Hawkin, who hadn't thought they could sober up Wintering, gazed dispassionately at their handiwork and was now convinced it could be done like that, in such short order, but at a cost he would just as soon never have to experience. But at least it was done, so now he could think of other things: Constable Beckman for instance, and the local procedure for holding a coroner's inquest. Taylor had sat through dozens of those hearings, but never south of Colorado. Experience had taught him long ago that not only did each community have its particular variations, but each State and Territory did also.

He was thinking of hunting up the town marshal when Pres said, 'Someone had ought to stay with Pete.' He did not elaborate. Perhaps he meant because Wintering looked ill, and perhaps he meant someone should be around to help the ashen liveryman if the Durants came looking for the only witness to the killing of a Durant.

Taylor and Ham looked at the saloonman without commenting, and Pres seemed to read something from their faces because he said, 'Come along, Pete. You can lie down in my backroom for an hour or so before the hearing commences. Maybe I can even find you some milk.'

Wintering was agreeable but when he arose he broke into a fresh sweat, and as they left his harness-room he walked somewhat feebly.

Ham went to the edge of the roadway beside Taylor Hawkin. They stood out there watching. No one had mentioned meeting again at the firehouse. No plans of any kind had been made. The four of them were allies, in a loose way, and perhaps each one thought that was all they needed.

The hostler Pete Wintering had dismissed earlier crept forth, pitchfork in hand, to also stand and watch as the rugged saloonman guided Wintering along. The hostler wagged his head. It was the first time he had ever seen Pete Wintering, who was by nature a strongly independent, self-reliant individual, look that bad.

A pair of dust-covered horsemen walked their lean horses southward down the roadway, grinning. They too had seen the saloonman and Wintering, and from the middle of the thoroughfare they had guessed what Wintering's trouble was.

They did not tarry. Evidently they were some of the itinerant rangemen who would be filtering down through the mesa country for the next few months on their way to familiar ranges, most probably, where they had the promise of employment from cow outfits they had worked for the previous year.

Up the roadway, on the west side out front of Jake Rowan's corral-yard, a small clutch of men were working over either a wheel or an axle, on a jacked-up stagecoach. Whatever repair they were making was probably minor because the three passengers, two salesmen and an older woman, were part of the interested crowd, and from time to time the pedlars offered advice. It was a relaxed group, which it would not have been if the damage had been serious. Most likely one of the leather grease-seals had worn through and was now being replaced.

Otherwise, the town seemed the same. It was difficult to imagine folks knew the riders from Faro Canyon were coming.

Ham said, 'Uncle Jake would be disappointed.'

Taylor offered no statement so the younger man explained out of hand.

'My paw died six years back. His brother's head of the clan. My paw was a pretty easy-going feller but Uncle Jake sort of likes the idea of folks up here on the mesa looking a little out where the riders from down in the canyon are concerned. Not exactly a bully, but Uncle Jake believes in folks having respect.'

To Taylor the distinction was finely-drawn between being a bully and not, in this instance, so he cocked a critical eye at the younger man, but said nothing.

Across where the gunsmith had his shop an older man strolled forth, looked left and right as though seeking something or someone, ran thick thumbs beneath the black suspenders holding up his trousers, gave them a light flip and turned back into the shop.

Someone else did that; Frank Beckman walked into the roadway and looked up and down, but Frank had a clear reason to be concerned and both the men down in front of the livery-barn understood Beckman's anxiety.

Ham said, 'Well hell; let's go up where they'll be holding the hearing.' He too peered up the north roadway. 'The family had ought to be along directly now.'

Taylor did not budge. 'Ham,' he said in a mildly remonstrating tone.

Young Durant's perception was excellent. 'Marshal, you need all the help you can get. We already talked about this, and my notions are no different now than they were before.' Ham stood his ground. 'About half the time I'm in Dutch with the family anyway.' He grinned a little. 'What's one more time?'

They started out of the yard and across to the opposite plankwalk where they headed northward. The firehouse was north of Pres Lynch's saloon several doors. It was not exclusively a firehouse. It was also a community building. Rarely did a fire break out in town, and because most structures were made of huge old logs fires had trouble getting a good start, nor did the vigilance of a community which really only had fire to fear, offer much opportunity for fire. Inside every doorway of the stores up and down Main Street were two red buckets, one containing sand, one containing water. When someone blew the fire-horn men loped forth with a red bucket in each hand.

Otherwise, the firehouse was also the place where people celebrated Independence Day on the 4th of July, Hallow'en, Christmas, Thanksgiving Day, and between those national holidays, held spring and summer and harvest dances.

Here, also, Holt township had been holding court hearings for a full generation. There was a lot of precedent, but very little of it in the case of someone being involved from Faro Canyon.

Chapter Thirteen

A THREATENED TOWN

They had reached the firehouse and in fact were turning to push past the big ajar door, when someone up the road made a loud, long whistling sound, and Taylor sensed the warning in the sound and turned back. Ham too stepped to the edge of the plankwalk.

The horsemen were distant and they were advancing slowly. Taylor thought this had to be part of someone's strategy. Maybe Uncle Jake Durant's strategy. It would make a greater impression if the riders from Faro Canyon advanced upon the town in a big armed group, slowly, in order that everyone would have ample time to see them and to be sobered by their approach.

Ham confirmed all this by quietly saying, 'Well hell; that's my older brother Job to the left, and the bearded feller in the centre, that's my uncle.'

Behind Taylor a man said, 'I thought when you left town last night, Marshal, you weren't coming back.'

Taylor turned and eyed Constable Beckman for a thoughtful moment before answering him. 'Sorry to disappoint you.'

Ham only glanced briefly over his shoulder, then returned to watching those oncoming riders. He did not seem particularly worried although he certainly had a right to be worried.

Southward down the roadway people were along both sides of the road, looking northward. As the men from Faro Canyon got closer those spectators drifted away, some to take refuge in stores and some to prudently head for home where they would stay.

Word travelled; Pres stepped out of the saloon and looked, then went back inside. At Rowan's stage-station a stooped man wearing a green eye-shade also came out for one look, and retreated, but down by the log gate of the yard itself Rowan and three of his yardmen stood in the gateway commenting. They did not vanish until the armed riders were almost to the edge of town.

Pres came forth again, wearing his hat and coat, turned to firmly lock the front doors of his saloon then go scuttling down the east plankwalk. It was easy to discern that Pres was wearing a shellbelt and gun under that coat. He ducked into the general store.

Ham said, 'Yeah, that's Uncle Jake's way all right,' and sounded slightly disgusted as he spoke.

Taylor turned. The south roadway was almost empty, now. Tethered horses had been led away, the stationary spectators had almost completely disappeared, and there were no riders passing along. In a doorway here and there a man or two stood peering, but these would no doubt also vanish when the Durants entered town.

Taylor eyed Frank Beckman from the corner of his eye. The constable looked pale as a ghost but resolute. For Taylor the question was: *how* resolute was Frank Beckman, and in which direction might he prove resolute? He would not be the first town marshal who had bowed to the menace of a bristling band of armed horsemen. It was impossible for Taylor to guess which way the local lawman would go.

In fact, when Taylor looked around, there was only one person in sight he felt would support him. Ham Durant, the one man among them all who perhaps shouldn't try to help him.

For a moment there was abundant reason for feeling that in remaining in Holt he might have made his last mistake, then he saw Preston Lynch emerge from the gunshop heading for the general store with the old gunsmith in tow. The gunsmith was carrying something Taylor had never seen before, a *three*-barrelled shotgun. It was not a bird-weapon; it was one of those scatterguns with barrels no more than two feet long. There was no weapon on the frontier which across the width of a roadway, or a room the size of the average saloon, inspired such respect. Someone ground-sluicing at close range with a short-barrelled shotgun could clean out an entire roomful with two blasts, and this unique weapon the old gunsmith was casually carrying in the crook of a bent arm, would still have one more barrel to threaten survivors with.

Pres looked northward. Maybe he saw Beckman, Ham Durant and Taylor Hawkin up in front of the firehouse — he probably did — but his interest was well past them up near the north edge of town where the men from the canyon were approaching.

Taylor said, 'Constable . . .' and jutted his jaw.

Frank turned, caught sight of Pres and the gunsmith, saw two other men step aside at the doorway of the general store, then hike on in behind the two armed townsmen, and groaned.

'All we'll need, by gawd, is for Pres and

those confounded vigilantes of his to show up at the firehouse loaded for bear.'

Ham ignored the constable to say, 'What in the hell . . . that's my sister!'

His astonishment was no less than Frank Beckman's surprise when the armed riders got close enough to the north edge of town to be recognizable. Frank said, 'What is Jake thinking of to allow that?'

Ham concurred. 'Or Job. Or any of the others.'

Taylor did not recognize her right away because she was in the second row, sandwiched between a pair of her stalwart brothers, but eventually he could see her.

She did not appear to be armed, at least there was no Winchester butt alongside the fork of her saddle and there did not appear to be a bulletbelt around her small waist, but Taylor had learned his lesson about these Durants; they could be armed when they least appeared to be.

Also, she was wearing a floppy hat with the brim pulled low to shield her eyes from sunglare, and perhaps because when she had left the canyon this morning it had been cold down there, she was also wearing a worn, large old jacket.

His interest in her arrival, though, was interrupted twice, once by Ham swearing with feeling over her being there at all, and again when Frank Beckman said, 'I never figured Jake would hold still for anything like this. He's went and put her in the worst possible position, Ham . . . ?'

Young Durant snarled. 'What do you expect me to do about it, Frank? I agree with you, but I'm not going up there on foot and try to make her go back. Look at Job; when he's got that expression on his face . . . Look at my other brothers.'

Taylor Hawkin could almost have put forth a hand and pressed against the mounting agitation and tension surrounding the three of them.

Down at the livery-barn a man rode forth on a sleek big black horse, sat a moment in the roadway gazing northward, then wheeled the black and headed southward out of town.

Evidently that worried dayman had decided to make a run for it after all, even though as Pete Wintering had said, no one cared about him because he was not involved.

Some men just naturally felt threatened by any kind of imminent danger.

Frank Beckman said, 'The damned fool,' and turned his back.

Ham's interest was still northward. He fi-

nally let his breath out noisily. The appearance of his sister among the riders
approaching town was a blow. 'I can't understand it,' he exclaimed. 'I can't understand Uncle Jake allowing it.'

Taylor craned southward. Now, the full
length of the roadway was empty. Whatever
Pres Lynch was up to, there was no sign of
him now, nor of the old gunsmith with his
triple-threat scattergun. Taylor faced Constable Beckman.

'You think they'll start trouble as soon as
they get down here?'

Frank shook his head. 'Just scare the whey
out of everybody is all. That's what they're
doin' now, coming into town in a big bunch
with guns all over 'em. But they won't make
trouble. Not until after the hearing, or
maybe during it . . . Ham?'

Young Durant concurred. 'Trouble will
come after you're acquitted, Marshal. *If*
you're acquitted.'

'It won't matter if the acquittal is fair?'
asked Taylor, and did not get an answer
from either of his companions. Southward,
someone called up the roadway. They
turned.

That livery-barn hostler on the black
horse was walking his handsome big mount
back into town. A couple of hundred yards

below him spread out across the stageroad on both sides, were eleven more armed horsemen. Taylor could count this contingent because they were strung out.

They had clearly turned back the hostler, had swept him slowly back into town as they advanced.

Taylor did not need Frank Beckman's exclamation to make a guess about this fresh band of horsemen. Frank said, 'Croslys, by gawd!'

Pete Wintering had predicted down at the harness-room of his livery-barn this would happen, and now it had.

Taylor roughly guessed there were nine Durants, including Barbara. That made a total of twenty hostile riders from Faro Canyon. Another time he might have been impressed by the closing jaws of the deliberate Faro Canyon tactic, right now his concern was a whole lot more individually personal, and the idea recurred that he had made an irreversible mistake. Then Ham said something reassuring.

'Uncle Jake isn't going to make trouble with Barb along.'

Frank agreed with that, but Taylor had always felt slightly reserved towards the town marshal. It had seemed to Taylor over the times he had been around Beckman, that he either wished so hard for the best that he seemed to believe in it explicitly, or else went to the other extreme and turned bleak and bitter over the prospects of disastrous trouble. Right now Frank wanted to believe the leader of the Durant clan would not make trouble, so he agreed when Ham speculated.

Beckman glanced around, then said, 'No point in us standing out here.' He fished for his pocket-watch, opened the case and looked intently at the little black hands. 'Quarter to ten and court convenes at ten.' He snapped the watch closed, pocketed it and cast a final glance up the roadway. 'I can use some help inside,' he said, and led the way.

Ham followed Taylor Hawkin into the firehouse where it was cool, and where there was a noticeable scent of oiled flooring.

The room had fire-fighting equipment from leather buckets to red-handled fire-axes along both walls, east and west, but up front with the flag on a pole shoved into a wooden stand, someone had pushed and pulled a large dark table into position and had flanked it with several chairs.

Otherwise, benches had been set up in rows, and along the east side of the room three rows of chairs had been arranged for a jury. Frank Beckman had been busy all morning, right up until he'd walked forth to stare at the approaching men from the canyon, and if he had made all these laborious arrangements by himself, he had managed to accomplish a lot more than Taylor would have expected from him.

There was a big photograph of the late President on the south wall behind the table. It was still draped with black bunting even though Abraham Lincoln had been killed many years earlier.

There were two smaller pictures flanking the big Lincoln picture. One was of General Grant, and the other one was of General Lee whom Grant had beaten in the War Between The States.

Frank looked at his pocket-watch again, from up by the south end of the room where the presiding magistrate — himself — would order the proceedings, and it was hard for Taylor Hawkin to decide whether the constable was calmly viewing his arrangements of the court for any possible last-minute arrangements, or whether Frank was badly shaken and uncertain.

Ham caught Taylor's look and leaned to quietly say, 'Don't toss him to the wolves just yet.'

Whatever that meant, Taylor only

guessed and Ham did not try to explain. Out front, they heard a man's deep voice grumble like distant thunder, and Ham looked a little anxious for the first time.

'Uncle Jake,' he muttered, and removed the empty sixgun holster he was still wearing, draped it by the belt from a peg in the rear of the room, then tendered a smile to Taylor which seemed to be shy just a little of Ham's former confidence. Not very much, just a little, and that was reassuring to Taylor who had only this much visual evidence that he was not alone.

Constable Beckman snapped his watch closed, strode to the south end of the room, placed his hat upon the table and with his back to the younger man, drew his Colt and also placed it upon the table, atop a thick old dog-eared lawbook.

Chapter Fourteen

THE FIREHOUSE

Trials even when they amounted to nothing more than coroner's inquests, usually drew large crowds in most small towns and Holt was no exception. But this morning the time for people to hasten forward, if they wanted seats, arrived and departed, and the only people to enter the firehouse were a party of armed men, with a girl among them, led by a large, bearded, grizzled man whose hooded pale eyes looked stonily from Constable Beckman up near the front of the room, to Hamilton Durant standing unarmed and watchful, near an equally as tall, but older, armed man.

To Taylor Jake Durant fitted the idea he had formed of a patriarch. Jake was large, and although he was now old and thicker than he had once been, there was ample evidence that at one time Jake Durant had been a man to step warily around.

He still looked menacing, but perhaps that was because of this particular occasion.

The other Durants ranged in age from within a year or two of Ham's age, to about ten or twelve years older, and they were all large men, except for a thick, broad Durant who was slightly shorter than his brothers.

Barbara also stared across where Ham and Taylor were. Her face showed nothing. She met Taylor's gaze frankly but did not change expression when she saw him. She did not look pleased at seeing Ham over there, either. Taylor decided that this was another case where someone's stony impassivity made it impossible to arrive at even a clue concerning their inner emotions. But in Barbara's case he *thought* he understood; at least he *hoped* he understood.

Constable Beckman seated himself at the flag-flanked table, put aside his hat, clasped both hands and stared back where the men from Faro Canyon were crowding inside.

'Park all weapons,' he called. 'You can hang gunbelts on the hooks along the back wall where you'd hang your hats.'

Frank's voice echoed. He sat hunched forward a little, still with his hands clasped together in front of him atop the table, looking steadily at the armed newcomers who were spreading out along the back of the room. Frank was waiting for that edict about guns to be obeyed. Taylor almost pitied the constable. He had to be in the most uncomfortable situation of his life-time, and aside from that if the Durants decided to ignore Beckman's mandate about putting aside all weapons there was not going to be very much Frank could do about it. Not by himself.

He finally rapped the tabletop and said, 'Be seated. Court will convene.' He paused, still hunched forward. 'Court will be convened, gents, as soon as you've complied with the town ordinance against wearing guns during proceedings.'

Taylor leaned against the east wall, hands at his sides, watching. The stalwart man Ham had identified as his brother Job looked to be a sort of leader, perhaps second-in-command under his uncle. All the Durant men were noticeably alike in build. Almost all of them. And they had distinctive characteristics which made them identifiable as Durants. Generally, they were fair. Even the ones with dark hair and eyes were not the least bit Latin in general look or build.

Barbara moved along the back wall with her brothers. She moved past them to reach the far end of their line. Here, she was fairly close to where Taylor Hawkin was standing. She looked past him at her brother, and

Ham smiled. She did not smile back, she was as solemn as an owl.

Several bold townsmen came in from the front roadway. There was a little head-nodding between the townsmen and the Durants but no talking. A townsman stepped to a wall peg, unslung his shellbelt and weapon, draped it from the peg, clapped his hat over both and turned to find a seat among the benches. He had done this as naturally as anyone might who had been through this procedure several times before and knew what was required of him.

The other townsmen did the same.

A few more people entered. So far they were all male. There was no conversation as the townsmen ranged along the wall hanging up the weapons they had entered with, although not all had come into the firehouse armed. Taylor wryly wondered how many of those men, who knew very well the condition in the firehouse, had hide-out guns.

A second large body of armed strangers walked in. They came as the Durants had arrived, all in a group. Taylor thought they were the Croslys and he was correct. He glanced at Ham and the younger man very slightly inclined his head as though in response to Taylor's question.

The Croslys were distinctive too, but in attire and general bearing they very closely resembled the Durants. Clearly, these two clans had evolved together down in their private cattle empire, many of their characteristics blending.

It was difficult for Taylor to determine which of the Croslys was Uncle Jake's equivalent as leader of the Crosly clan. There were several who seemed to be men of authority. Generally, the Croslys were a little darker and not quite so tall and stalwart, but beyond making a few obvious observations Taylor arrived at no general nor sweeping conclusions about these men whom he was viewing for the first time.

One of them, a greying, rather handsome man, said, 'Constable, where's the prisoner?'

Taylor stiffened a little. Frank Beckman nodded in the direction of the east wall. 'There is the *defendant*, Jeff.'

The armed men all turned, and the greying man called Jeff finished his study of Taylor then said, 'Constable — he's armed.'

Beckman had an answer ready. 'So are you, Jeff. So is just about everyone else in here.' Beckman looked at Taylor. 'Marshal, we got an ordinance . . .'

Taylor reached to unbuckle his gunbelt, then he stepped up beside Barbara Durant to hang the weapon from a peg, and to place his hat over the belt too. Without looking down he softly said, 'You shouldn't be here.'

She said nothing. She was looking directly ahead and continued to do that.

Ham looked at Jeff Crosly. 'Well . . . ?' he said quietly.

Jeff began to work loose his gunbelt and as he did so he grumbled to the other Croslys around him. That started it. Jake Durant who was being watched by the Durants on both sides of him, nodded. Taylor thought he did it grudgingly.

Frank Beckman was undoubtedly relieved. If they had not disarmed themselves he could not have done it. Taylor considered Jeff Crosly. It seemed to him that if he had to rely upon fairness from someone he did not know, it might be this dark-eyed man.

Frank Beckman pointed. 'Marshal; that's your chair.'

Taylor walked over, sat, and looked around. Ham was still over along the east wall, thick arms folded, but in Taylor's place beside him now, Barbara was standing.

Beckman struck the tabletop. 'Be seated,' he called, and amid the noise of all those men seeking places along the benches Jake Durant said something to Jeff Crosly, and the darker man shrugged his shoulders.

A few more bold townspeople filtered through from out front. For the first time there were a few women. They were escorted by their menfolk, and when these people saw Barbara Durant over beside her brother, they stared. They all evidently knew who she was but had no more expected to see her here today than her brother had.

At the door, several men shouldered through. Taylor heard the scuffling and looked. So did Constable Beckman, and he pointed as the newcomers pushed on inside.

'Jury there,' Frank said, pointing. 'Witness up here . . . Pete, you don't look right well.'

Wintering shuffled ahead of the men he had arrived with, and glared. 'I don't feel right well,' he growled at Frank Beckman. 'Who would, in this place!'

The jurymen avoided looking at anyone, it seemed to Taylor Hawkin, as they filed to their chairs. One of them was Pres Lynch, to Taylor's surprise, another one was Jake Rowan with his head cocked to one side and upwards. The others Taylor had seen around town but did not know.

Pres Lynch was armed. Taylor would

have wagered his bay horse on it. Pres was still wearing that full frock coat, and nothing hid a holstered Colt as well.

Back near the rear of the room an older man leaned to close the door. When he faced back around Taylor recognized him, too. It was the gunsmith he'd seen earlier crossing the road with that unique scattergun, and the old man had his sawed-off weapon cradled in one arm now as he looked calmly in the direction of Frank Beckman, and Frank returned that gaze just as calmly.

It did not occur to Taylor that the gun-smith might be justified in bringing his blunderbuss into the firehouse until Beckman said. 'Bailiff; court's convened. No one's to enter nor leave.'

The gunsmith answered flatly. 'They won't.'

Beckman cleared his throat, sat a moment gazing around, cracked his knuckles then launched into a preamble. 'Folks; you know me, I'm Frank Beckman constable of Holt Township.' He let that sink in before also saying, 'I'm authorized under Territorial law to sit as Justice Court Magistrate when there isn't a duly elected nor appointed one around. Today, we're not trying anyone. This isn't a trial, folks, it's a hearing, and if you don't know the difference see me later and I'll explain, but right now let's get down to brass tacks.'

Frank looked at Taylor Hawkin. 'Stand up and identify yourself,' he ordered.

Taylor arose, saw all those hard, hostile faces and swallowed. 'My name is Taylor Hawkin, I'm a Deputy U.S. Marshal out of Cheyenne, Wyoming, who also works under the U.S. Marshal in Denver. I have a warrant for the arrest of one Bart McClelland — also known as Bart Durant. The charge is bank robbery and murder. I left Denver two days late and didn't catch up to McClelland-Durant until a couple of days ago, down here. I was standing with my back to him in the livery-barn, with the liveryman, when he called me. The liveryman was a witness. Bart started his draw and I shot him.'

Taylor remained standing for a moment, and when there was not a sound in the room, he finally resumed his seat.

Constable Beckman rapped the tabletop for attention. 'That's the federal officer's story. Mister Wintering the liveryman will now stand and tell his version of that gunfight.'

Pete did not look as bad as he had looked several hours earlier down at the harness-room, but he did not look ready to run anyone a foot-race either. He stood, looked around, and perhaps because he did not feel very good he was brusque when he said, 'That's exactly how it happened. Bart said something to the marshal about he'd have killed him a night or two earlier if he could have got a sighting on him. Then he said he'd do it now — something like that — and started his draw.'

There was not a sound. Constable Beckman waited a suitable time then prompted Wintering. 'What's the rest of it, Pete?'

'You know darned well what the rest of it is,' growled the unhappy liveryman, glaring. 'I told you, Frank, that Bart Durant was never in his best days in the marshal's class with a gun. He had his gun half out, no more'n two-thirds out. He just plain was outgunned. He never completed that draw before the marshal cut him down dead as a stone in my livery-barn runway.' Pete looked steadily at craggy, bearded Jake Durant. 'It was a fair fight,' he stated slowly, spacing out the words. 'A — fair — fight!'

Beckman said, 'Thank you and sit down.' He ranged a searching look around the silent room. 'The bench will entertain questions,' he announced, looking straight at Jake Durant.

Job arose, Ham's elder brother, a massive, powerful, taciturn man. 'One witness isn't as good as three or four,' he said to Constable Beckman. 'Folks have been known to buy just one witness, Frank.'

Beckman cleared his throat again as Job reseated himself. He looked at Taylor Hawkin, then back to Job. 'We only have one witness,' he announced. 'That's the way it happened, Job. Pete was the only one to see that killing. We got to live with that.'

Job started to rise, to speak again, but Frank Beckman rapped the tabletop and spoke first. 'I told you folks, this isn't a trial, it's a hearing. All we got to do here is determine whether or not there is enough evidence to warrant me locking up the deputy U.S. marshal and holding him until we can get a circuit-riding judge up here to hold a real trial.' Beckman let that soak in before also saying, 'You boys on the jury — questions?'

Jake Rowan had a question. 'Does the deputy marshal have official orders?'

Beckman looked at Taylor, and the latter nodded his head so Beckman said, 'Stand up, Deputy, and read 'em to the jury!'

Chapter Fifteen

THE VERDICT!

Taylor's orders from the U.S. Marshal up north were bluntly explicit. He was to pursue the killer known as Bart McClelland until he caught up to him, then he was to apprehend him, 'using his own discretion as to the best way of accomplishing the apprehension'.

Taylor lowered the paper and looked slowly along the rows of lifted faces. 'I've gone after my share of fugitives, gents, and I've never yet shot one if it was possible not to have to do it. As for this man I killed in your town — I had an idea he wasn't named McClelland when I left Denver, but that's all I knew until I got down here. But that wouldn't have made much difference if I could have taken him alive. I'd have extradited him back to Denver.' He continued to look at them. 'I have the allegations concerning his crime, if you want to hear them.'

Jake Durant gravely inclined his head. So did Pres Lynch among the jurors, as well as that dark-eyed man called Jeff Crosly.

Taylor looked at Frank Beckman and the constable acted resigned.

'All right, read it,' he said.

'There were four witnesses inside the bank,' stated Taylor, and read their depositions one by one, reading slowly without any special emphasis. When he was finished he turned from the waist and looked steadily at Ham, then at his sister. She had been watching Taylor throughout. Now, he thought she looked relieved, or perhaps it was just resigned, he could not be sure.

Jake Rowan had another question, his sly gaze fixed upon the federal lawman. 'How'd it come that you got Ham Durant on your side, Marshal?'

Frank Beckman reddened. 'Jake, you *listen,* you don't interrogate — you're a juryman, not a prosecutor nor a magistrate.'

Rowan's sly glance drifted around the room as though to imply that he'd been silenced while upon the verge of forcing some kind of an admission. Taylor did not believe Rowan liked him, and he knew for a fact that Rowan was one of those people who enjoyed stirring up trouble. In order to squelch suspicions before they got well formed, Taylor answered Rowan's question.

'Last night I went down to Faro Canyon.'

He paused to look at Ham, then back towards the upturned faces of the roomful of spectators. 'I got lucky and caught Hamilton Durant flat-footed and brought him up here as my hostage to make certain the Durants didn't try to clean me out before I had a chance to tell my side of that killing in the livery-barn.' Taylor looked at Frank, who nodded, then Taylor sat down.

Jake Rowan looked as though he were going to speak, but Pres Lynch next to him jammed a bony elbow into the stage-company executive's side and Jake gasped.

Frank Beckman struck his tabletop again, something he appeared to feel inclined to do whenever a particular aspect of the hearing had been completed to his satisfaction.

Now, he said, 'Folks; as nearly as I can figure out, that is the entire matter, so I'll now charge the jury.'

A calm, strong voice from over along the east side of the room spoke up. 'There is one more thing,' Barbara Durant said, looking over the heads of her brothers and the others, looking directly at Constable Beckman.

'Bart knew the deputy marshal was after him. He came down into Faro Canyon the evening before. I met him out in the yard at the ranch. No one else was around. We talked for a little while and I told him he'd ridden his horse too hard . . . He told me about the U.S. marshal behind him. He said for me to keep close watch and when I saw that marshal to head for town and let him know — so he could set up a surprise for the marshal.'

Barbara stopped speaking. She did not look in Taylor's direction but he had his glance fixed upon her as did most of the other people in the room, including her uncle and her elder brother Job.

'I didn't ride up and warn him,' she said softly.

Constable Beckman was leaning forward as he said, 'You had a reason, Barbara?'

She answered softly. 'Yes, I had a reason . . . I've known Bart all my life. Everyone in this room knew him. While we were talking in the yard I asked him what he'd done. He said . . . an old man got in his way up in Denver and he'd shot him . . . Then he said a woman had tried to stop him as he was leaving a bank so he'd blown her away too.'

Barbara Durant gazed at her uncle. Several of her brothers looked back and forth between them. Her uncle showed nothing as he returned her stare. Finally she faced Constable Beckman.

'I met the deputy U.S. marshal the next

morning down in the canyon . . . Mister Beckman I knew what would happen to him. I also guessed what might happen if I didn't warn Bart . . . Like I said, I've known Bart all my life, we all have. Maybe folks will blame me for his death because I didn't ride up and tell him the marshal was on his way to Holt . . . I didn't *know* Bart would get killed if I didn't ride up here, but I knew exactly what would happen to the marshal if I came up here. He'd bushwhack him.'

There was a sharp intake of breath among the Durants. It occurred to Taylor Hawkin that probably no one had ever before called one of them a bushwhacker. Certainly no Durant had ever said that about another Durant before.

Barbara swung to face her brothers, and now her eyes showed steady warmth. 'Are we all supposed to pretend we didn't know Bart?'

Jake looked away and Taylor had the impression he was less irate than chagrined. Taylor swung to shoot a look at Ham. The younger Durant was still standing with mighty arms folded, beside his sister. He was watching his uncle as though what his sister had just said had particularly needed saying.

Frank Beckman faced the jurymen.

'Gents; that's it. What you just heard don't have much to do with what you've been impanelled about — which is: did the U.S. deputy marshal justifiably shoot and kill Bart Durant, or didn't he? That's all you got to decide, then tell me. If he did, this here hearing will end the affair and there won't be any trial. If he *was not* justified then when you so tell me, I'll lock him up and arrange for a formal trial.' Frank waited a moment before finally saying, 'Turn around and keep your voices down, and have your palaver. Take as much time as you want.' Frank looked at his watch, looked around the room, and threw a glance far back where the gunsmith was still leaning with his shotgun cradled in his arms. 'If any of 'em want to go outside now, they can, providing they aren't jurymen, the witness or the U.S. lawman.'

No one budged.

For a long while the room buzzed with a low undertone of conversation over among the huddled jurymen and also among the spectators. Taylor saw that dark-eyed Crosly, the one called Jeff, rise from his place among the benches and make his way slowly back where Jake Durant was sitting. Several of the younger Durants pushed over to make room.

Jake and Jeff bowed their heads in solemn conversation. To Taylor it could have been the meeting of a pair of people making plans to hang him, or even to have him shot down in the roadway if he was acquitted and walked forth into the sunshine of the roadway.

It could also be something entirely different. If there was something to pin a hope upon, Taylor decided it was that man named Crosly. He at least had never seemed openly hostile.

Jake Rowan turned and tapped Taylor on the shoulder. 'You ever shoot a fugitive before?' he hissed, but Frank Beckman saw and called out sharply.

'I told you, Jake, confound it — you listen. That's your job as a juryman. If you got a question you ask the bench — which is me — and if the bench figures it should be answered the bench'll rephrase it. What was it you wanted to know?'

'Did this U.S. marshal ever shoot a fugitive before?' asked Rowan, his crooked neck making the look he raised to Frank Beckman seem more sly than dispassionate.

Frank's eyes flashed. 'For the last time,' he exclaimed, 'I'll tell you, Jake: we are not trying this man. We are figuring out whether or not he acted justifiably. As for what he might have done somewhere else — damn it all — we can only hold a hearing for what he did *here*. That's how the law reads. A man can't be tried at the same time for but one crime and in this kind of a hearing you can't even try and make out that he's maybe killed someone else. It's just this one case, right here in our town, we're concerned about and nothing else. Jake?'

'All right,' stated Rowan, and turned his back to rejoin the huddling jurors.

Frank and Pete Wintering exchanged a look. Pete shook his head in candid disgust.

Someone walked over and leaned down behind Taylor. He felt the presence and twisted to raise his head. Ham Durant winked at him and softly said, 'It's lookin' better.'

Not to Taylor Hawkin it wasn't looking better. He squared forward on the chair. Men studied him from among the spectators, their faces showing cautious interest. Not all of them looked encouraging. Three or four of them looked openly antagonistic but these were not all Durants, they were scattered among the roomful of people. He hadn't expected anything less. In fact, while Rowan was trying to make trouble for him a while back he had seen several other hostile looks directed in his direction.

Even if the jurymen found in his favour and said there was insufficient evidence of wrongdoing to hold him for an official trial, he still had to walk out of this building, and he still had to saddle up and ride out of this territory.

Preston Lynch hauled himself back around on the chair, and smoothed his coat. As he did this Taylor caught a glimpse of a walnut gunstock. So, evidently, did Frank Beckman because he scowled and said, 'Pres, did you forget to shed your pistol?'

Lynch blinked, reddened, then offered a weak smile. 'Plumb forgot for a fact,' he mumbled, and several men among the spectators snickered.

Frank struck his desktop for silence. Everyone watched the saloonman go back and drape his gunbelt from a wall peg, then return to his seat, red in the face and unwilling to meet the spectators yet, so he concentrated on the constable.

'We got a verdict,' he announced, buttoning his coat to rise.

Frank Beckman struck his tabletop. 'Silence,' he called around the room where no one was making a sound and where every eye was upon the standing man with the scarred, rugged countenance.

'What is your finding, Pres?'

'Justifiable self-defence, Frank.'

If there was surprise no one made any kind of gasp or curse to indicate it.

'Is that a unanimous verdict?' asked Beckman, and Pres Lynch pursed his lips a moment as though carefully considering his answer before giving it.

'Yes, it was unanimous, Frank,' he ultimately retorted, 'but there was a couple of fellers had to be talked to pretty nasty to get them to make it unanimous.'

Someone laughed. Frank Beckman was outraged and struck his desktop harder than he had done at any other time since the beginning of the hearing, but he could not determine who had laughed because the offending individual immediately became contrite and frozen-faced so that he would blend with everyone else, and it worked.

Pres Lynch remained standing. He looked uncomfortably self-conscious and he was.

Taylor Hawkin swung to look at Ham, then to Barbara. For the first time since entering the firehouse she looked squarely at him with an expression which was not blank. She smiled at him.

Frank said, 'That's the end of it, then. Folks, Deputy U.S. Marshal Taylor Hawkin has been found innocent of committing a crime; it's been decided by the jury that he acted justifiably — and I'll be darned if I could see how they could hand down any other verdict.'

Frank stood up, neglected to strike his tabletop, and said, 'That's all, folks. It's over and done with.' He looked steadily at Jake Durant. 'Even if some of you don't agree, just remember this: in the eyes of the law Marshal Hawkin is a free man, and if you look for trouble with him . . . aside from the fact that the law won't tolerate it, there might be some good advice in remembering what Pete said. Marshal Hawkin was far too fast for Bart. And they tell me Bart wasn't slow with a gun.' Frank continued to eye Jake Durant as the spectators rose to file outside. He had clearly been offering a clear-cut warning to the leader of the Durants.

Chapter Sixteen

THE OUTCOME

Hamilton Durant and Barbara walked against the tide of departing spectators over to Taylor's chair. As he arose to return the handsome girl's smile, her brother said, 'Darned if I could see how they could go any other way.' He extended a big hand and Taylor briefly shook it.

He would have spoken to Barbara but Pres Lynch walked over, buckling his bulletbelt and sixgun around his middle again, beneath the dark coat. Pres did not smile, exactly, but his eyes had a hard twinkle in their depths. He nodded at Barbara then ignored her in Taylor's favour.

'That is that,' said Pres, with a strong note of finality in his voice. 'If you'd care to drop round to my place, I'll set 'em up a couple of times.'

Taylor's response was predictable. 'I'm obliged, and I'm mighty relieved about that verdict,' he said. 'I'll likely come by your bar later on.'

Pres departed and Taylor turned again to speak to the handsome girl. Constable Beckman approached from the rear with a comment.

'Had to be,' he told them. 'Had to be that verdict, and I never doubted but that they'd hand it in.' He did not offer his hand and he did not smile at the acquitted lawman. 'Lots of things we don't have here in Holt,' he exclaimed, 'but by gawd there is one thing we *do* have — plain justice.'

Frank bobbed his head and turned away as Pete Wintering came over. Pete still looked peaked and pale, but evidently he was feeling better and in fact he was more alert now than he had been.

'After all the misery you boys give me this morning if I'd been on that jury I'd have hanged you,' he told Taylor frankly, then glanced at Barbara. 'Took spirit what you did, missy, speakin' up like that in a roomful of men, and sort of against the Durants. I admire you for it.'

Three stalwart men walked quietly back into the room over by the doorway, and stood there gazing in Taylor's direction. Two of them were Durants and one was a Crosly. They were armed.

Taylor saw them, guessed their interest was in him, and surmised that they had come looking for him to be certain he had not fled the firehouse by some other exit. They stood over there slouched and easy, hands hooked in bulletbelts.

Ham saw them too, but until Wintering trudged doorward Ham made no mention of what seemed to Taylor Hawkin to be a quiet menace.

Barbara, following the eyes of her brother and Taylor, turned to look. She faced forward with a comment. 'What do *they* want, Ham? Mister Beckman warned them.'

The only way to answer Barbara was to go back there and find out what they wanted. Taylor started for the door with Ham behind him. Before they completed their crossing of the long room Constable Beckman poked his head in, saw the waiting armed men from Faro Canyon, and stepped fully into the doorway to say, 'What are you fellers up to? There's not going to be any trouble, you understand that? Walk out of there and go on over across the road where the rest of the Faro Canyon folks is standing with their horses.'

The three men swung their attention to Constable Beckman without moving or speaking. Frank had probably never really intimidated a rider from Faro Canyon. When they had obeyed him in the past it had been because the patriarchs down in the canyon had said he was to be respected.

Now, they remained relaxed in place eyeing Frank as though they had not quite made up their minds whether to heed him or not.

Taylor pushed past Hamilton and widened his stride in order to get over there first. When he was only the width of two bench-rows distant he said, 'What did you have in mind, fellers?'

They looked forward again. Behind Taylor their younger brother bristled. 'Ulysses, what's wrong with you? You heard that verdict. Vernon, you're not his match. What do you fellers want to do, get more Durants salted down?'

From an open window mid-way along the north side of the firehouse someone pulled steel over wood with a harsh sound. The old gunsmith with his blunderbuss was back there. Beside him, only his head and shoulders visible, was Pres Lynch. He called to the small knot of people over by the door. 'Break it up. You Durants: there's eleven vigilantes around the firehouse. You start anything and I'll promise you some dead Durants. *Turn around and walk the hell out of there!*'

Pres's command was obeyed. Ham's two

brothers and the other man from the canyon, marched forth into the sunlight. Ham shouldered past to walk out behind them, swearing at them under his breath.

In the brilliant daylight, over across the road, a large party of armed men stood beside their horses and watched. Elsewhere, along both plankwalks, townsmen stood resolutely with rifles, carbines, and belt-guns, it looked to Taylor Hawkin as though those 'vigilantes' as Frank Beckman had called them, were willing to face down the men from Faro Canyon even though they were fewer in number.

Taylor stepped into sunlight out front of the firehouse behind the three men being driven along ahead of him. Ham was on one side, Barbara was on the other side. Of the trio only Taylor was armed, but he might just as well not have been if there were trouble; at least sixteen or eighteen slouching Faro Canyon riders were opposite him across the roadway. There was no chance of any solitary gunfighter emerging alive from that kind of a shoot-out.

Those two Durants who had been inside walked over, halted and spoke curtly to the bearded patriarch of the Durant clan, then walked in different directions to their horses. Taylor halted just short of the roadway, upon the plankwalk, waiting for Jake Durant to take whatever step he felt he had to take. Finally, Jeff Crosly ambled up and said something, then he and Jake started for the centre of the roadway, and Barbara, whose keenness was superior to most, leaned and said, 'There isn't going to be any trouble. Not real trouble anyway. Maybe Vernon and Ulysses didn't like you being turned loose, and maybe there will be one or two among the Croslys who won't like it either, but there's not going to be trouble.'

Taylor did not take his eyes off the advancing older men. He was willing to put faith in Barbara's judgement, but at the same time he remained closely watchful.

Jake and Jeff passed the centre of the road and kept walking. They got over within a few feet of where Taylor was standing and Jake said, 'Ham; you let this lawman whup you?'

Hamilton looked sulphurously at his uncle. 'No sir, I didn't *let* him whup me. I did just about everything I could think of to keep him from whupping me, Uncle Jake. But he did it anyway.'

'He's fifty, sixty pounds lighter,' reproved Uncle Jake, 'and he's older.'

Ham gave a death's-head smile. 'Uncle

Jake, send Job over and let him try his luck. He's the best of us — and I'll give you ten to one odds the lawman can whup him too.'

Barbara braced her uncle, and it must have been totally unexpected because Jake Durant's mouth fell open. She said, 'You're talking like little boys. Who can whip who. And what difference does it make, Uncle Jake, whether the marshal whipped Ham or not? What you want to do is lean your weight and authority on the marshal, isn't it? You and Uncle Jeff want to impress him while you have all the clans over across the road to back the pair of you up . . . Sometimes . . . you make me ashamed of you. *Both* of you!'

Jeff Crosly reddened but Jake Durant's gaze lingered on his niece as though seeing her for perhaps the first time. Then Jake cleared his throat, looked at Taylor and said, 'Not trying to cow you, Marshal, just letting you know us folks from Faro Canyon don't like intruders nor meddlers. That's all.'

It was a diluted version of the remonstrance Taylor had half expected. Instead of being called a 'killer' he had been called, mildly he thought, an 'intruder'. He studied the pair of older men for a moment before speaking to them.

'I'll say to you out here what I couldn't say back in the firehouse. I'm sorry I had to kill Bart. I didn't want to do it even when he pushed us into fighting. But it's done, and unless someone tries to stop me, I'll be riding out tomorrow . . . I won't intrude on you any more.'

Jake shifted his stance and tucked both thumbs into the lower little pockets of his old vest. He looked at Taylor for a long time without speaking. Jeff Crosly seemed to be less inhibited. He spoke up at once.

'You don't have to rush out of here, Marshal. Lie over a few days, take your time.'

Jeff was placating; he also seemed more friendly than Jake or any of the others. In fact Jeff Crosly seemed more friendly out here than he had seemed during the hearing in the firehouse.

Taylor thinly smiled. 'There are folks who'd just as soon I wasn't around,' he told the cowman. 'If I lie over, Mister Crosly, it might make trouble. You don't want any more killings any more than I do. But thanks anyway.'

Jeff Crosly was placated. He sighed, then turned on Jake Durant. 'Well; we've said it all haven't we? Might as well head out for the canyon.'

Jake acted deaf. He said, 'No one from

the canyon will make trouble. We've had all we needed of that.'

Taylor had a question for Jake Durant. 'Was it really that Bart had been killed, Mister Durant, or was it simply that someone had dared draw on *any* Durant that fired you up?'

Jake stroked his beard without answering. In the end he gravely inclined his head and turned to walk back across the roadway without answering the question.

Ham snorted, but neither did he speak.

As the men from Faro Canyon milled and talked, then finally stepped up across leather and split off, part going north-westerly towards the roadway into the canyon, the other part riding loosely southward down through town and out the far end in the direction of the Crosly-trail, Pres Lynch in the doorway of his saloon, a carbine held behind him out of sight, raised a coat-sleeve to mop off sweat, and looked tremendously relieved.

All those other vigilantes were also relieved. They remained resolute, at least in appearance, up and down the roadway on both sides, watching as the Crosly clan headed on down through town, but they too were relieved.

Taylor, like everyone else, stood for a long

while in silent relief, watching. Then he turned towards Barbara, but before he could speak Ham said, 'Sis, I'll take your horse down to Wintering's and stall it. If you're a mind to eat, I'll meet you down at the cafe in a few minutes.'

He looked from her to Taylor, turned without another word and struck out across the road.

Taylor turned again towards the girl, and behind them northward a couple of storefronts a large, grey woman primly holding both hands across a round stomach, stepped into a doorway and said, 'Miss Durant, if you'd like to set a spell we'd be right obliged to have you visit the store. You're bound to be plumb worn down, what with all you been through today.'

Taylor flapped his arms and rolled his eyes.

Chapter Seventeen

BARBARA!

Frank Beckman and the liveryman were arguing at Lynch's bar at the same time Taylor Hawkin was finishing up scrubbing and shaving out back of the livery-barn, over near the stone trough which serviced the public corrals.

Wintering was of the opinion that Frank should have protected Pete, as a respectable and tax-paying member of the community, from what had happened down at Wintering's harness-room earlier that morning, and Frank's position was that anyone who knew very well he was the only witness who might save someone from getting lynched, went ahead and got drunk regardless, deserved just about anything that happened to them — short of being shot or anything that final.

Pres listened for a while then made a face and turned to hike up his bar where townsmen were standing elbow-to-elbow.

For the first time within living memory

everyone had something particular to talk about. Not just the trial but also the way the townsmen had stood against the men of Faro Canyon. Of course there had been no showdown, and a few discerning individuals were grateful for that, being of the opinion that the townsmen would never have been able to survive a shoot-out with the rangemen, but since nothing that drastic had occurred it was possible for a few brazen townsmen to make exaggerated claims about what would have happened if there had been a fight. No one could deny either viewpoint.

Ham and his sister ate at the deserted cafe opposite the stage company's corral-yard, and talked quietly but fervently. The cafeman would have eavesdropped but one good look at the size of Hamilton Durant had discouraged him.

Finally, when Taylor strode up the plankwalk towards the cafe where he was to meet Barbara and her brother, Jake Rowan stepped from his office, head cocked quizzically, and smiled.

'Hope you make it,' he called to Taylor Hawkin. 'I know — folks aren't against you any more — but all the same you never can tell when you're going to ride past some big rocks and get bushwhacked. I'm not saying it'll happen, mind you, all I'm saying is —'

'Why the hell,' exclaimed Taylor, 'don't you just try to keep your coaches running on schedule, and leave off minding everyone else's business?'

He stepped to the edge of the plankwalk and angled towards the cafe.

Jake glared and moved his lips in fierce profanity.

Ham saw Taylor approaching from the cafe window and sought for an excuse to leave. He had already looked in on the horses so he couldn't use that. An inspiration made him tell his sister he had to go get his gun, and as he arose patting the empty holster, he smiled at her.

She gravely watched him, then turned slightly as Ham headed for the door. Taylor was just entering. Ham muttered something and hastened past. Taylor turned to watch in bewilderment. As he faced back around Barbara beckoned.

'Ham is well-meaning and big and clumsy,' she told Taylor, as he came to the table and pulled out Ham's abandoned chair. She looked at him. 'Whatever you did, it's an improvement, Taylor.'

'Shaved and scrubbed up and sort of got relaxed,' he explained, admiring her beauty.

'Are you truly going to ride out tomorrow?' she asked.

He was. That had been his intention even before the hearing had ended — providing of course the hearing had not gone against him. 'It's a long ride back,' he told her.

'But a beautiful time of the year for a ride like that,' she murmured. 'Up through the Rockies?'

'Yes. Couple of weeks of lying around mountain lakes fishing and sleeping and swimming and . . .'

She was looking at her hands atop the table. 'And watching the stars,' she finished for him. 'And laughing at the chipmunks and squirrels.' Her eyes swept up to his face. 'I've ridden part way into the back country with my brothers a time or two.'

He felt the stirring to life of something fresh, and a little unnerving, between them. He thought she was beautiful and he knew exactly what else he would like to think of, about her — with her — but this was only the second time they had been alone together. It was in fact only the second day when he had seen her. The other day had been that morning when they had shared his fry-bread.

He smiled. 'Trout and grouse instead of fry-bread, and maybe wild turkey in the high forest, then down the other side towards Denver . . . Barbara?'

She looked at the backs of her hands again, saying nothing for a while. He could see the small pulse in her neck strongly beating.

'Barbara . . . ?'

Without raising her eyes she said, 'Do you want me to, Taylor?'

He had no trouble answering that. 'More than anything else, yes.'

'Well . . . I want to.' She shot him a quick look then went back to studying the backs of her hands atop the table. 'Do you remember where your camp was at the north end of the canyon?'

'Yes.'

'And the trail northward from there up through those huge grey boulders?'

'Yes.'

'There is a clearing a mile beyond the boulders with a little spring in it, and some pine trees.'

He knew the place; remembered it very well because he had thought of camping there the evening of his arrival in Faro Canyon.

She raised her eyes to him again. 'I'll meet you there tomorrow morning two hours before sun-up . . . Are you sure you want me, Taylor?'

He did not know what to tell her that he had not already said, so he threw up his hands. 'Like I want breath and water and health, Barbara. Are *you* sure?'

She almost smiled. 'From that first time — in your camp before you even offered me the fry-bread.' She waited a moment, then arose.

He said, 'Barb; your family will come after us like a hang-rope posse. They'll want me for stealing you.'

'Let them,' she replied, still close to smiling. 'Ham showed me all the tricks hunted things used to hide their tracks. They'll never get close to us, Taylor. They'll never find us . . . But someday, if you were willing, we could return.'

He arose and went outside with her. She felt for his hand, squeezed it, hard, then looked up and said, 'Ham will help.'

'Does he know?'

'I'll tell him when I get my horse from the livery-barn, when we're riding back for the canyon. I'll tell him I can't ever smile again unless I can escape from Faro Canyon. He'll know. Ham will understand, and he knows how to cover tracks, too.' She soberly regarded his face. 'You'll be at the clearing come dawn tomorrow?'

He nodded. He would be at that clearing

186

waiting for her at dawn if he had to crawl the full distance from town down there on his hands and knees.

She walked off in the direction of the livery-barn. Ham was down there, out front with Pete Wintering. He saw his sister approaching, saw Taylor Hawkin farther back watching her, and Ham had an inkling.

For Taylor, each lengthening afternoon shadow put him that much closer to discreetly saddling up tonight and heading for the point of rendezvous. He felt no regret at all over leaving Holt Township.

We hope you have enjoyed this Large Print book. Other Thorndike, Wheeler or Chivers Press Large Print books are available at your library or directly from the publishers.

For more information about current and up-coming titles, please call or write, without obligation, to:

Publisher
Thorndike Press
295 Kennedy Memorial Drive
Waterville, ME   04901
Tel. (800) 223-1244

Or visit our Web site at:
www.gale.com/thorndike
www.gale.com/wheeler

OR

Chivers Large Print
published by BBC Audiobooks Ltd
St James House, The Square
Lower Bristol Road
Bath BA2 3SB
England
Tel. +44(0) 800 136919
email: bbcaudiobooks@bbc.co.uk
www.bbcaudiobooks.co.uk

All our Large Print titles are designed for easy reading, and all our books are made to last.